Lornamair

Dax Christopher

Lornamair

Cover illustration by Schilling Concepts

ISBN 978-0-988-9873-2-6

Please visit the author's website
www.daxchristopherbooks.com
for other works and contact information

Thank you so much for your
interest in Larnaman –

May she return to you
what was taken

                    Dax Christopher

This story is dedicated to your self respect.

In the beginning, there was love.

Imagine an island, balmy weather, and a sunset. Imagine a serene paradise, a paradise that has been offered to you and your companion to do with as you wished. What would you do? Cultivate? Develop? Perhaps, if you had need for food and better living conditions. But now, imagine that needs like those are not your concern. You do not eat, because you are never hungry. You do not seek shelter, because the elements never make you uncomfortable, and you are never tired. There is no one to govern, no society to impress, no reason to explore or expand—no need for anything but the love you have felt for your companion since the moment you were self-aware. The two of you, blissfully unaware of the passage of time, have no history, no future—only the moment, with no reason to ask why or what you are.

Eventually, someone will find your paradise. Despite your lack of needs, the human race is not one that can ever be satisfied. You will discover that the world does not, in fact, belong to the two of you, and that there are places and people that you never dreamed existed. Now what? The two of you will find a way to hide, unwilling to complicate the purity of love and uncertain about the nature of the newcomers. You will watch from a distance as generations of them come and go, and you will learn of the realities of aging and reproduction. You will witness the establishment of a small society, as the original half-dozen, over time, become several hundred. Staying out of sight will prove difficult, and eventually someone will notice you.

You will encounter a man while walking, and he will mistake you for a member of his own species, since your features are similar. It is then that you will realize that these people are not necessarily violent, and you will share this realization with your companion. Soon there will be discontentment, for now love has made room for curiosity in your companion's heart. Meanwhile, the man you saw has gone home and told his friends that he saw someone not of the tribe. Decades later he will see you again as you and your companion are attempting to learn the native language through observation, and he will notice that you have not aged a day. You will become a legend among the people, whose children will be taught that you are divine, and a sign of good fortune.

Still, you will keep your distance, preferring not to be seen, while your companion chooses to be closer and closer to their world. Soon the one you love will be nearly indistinguishable from the rest, having made a successful, although gradual, transition into this new society. And soon, you will feel forgotten. You will watch as your former companion hides his immortality and discovers the hedonistic pleasures of humanity, while you scream silently at the loss of the only thing you ever had—love.

Imagine, now, that you want to die, and cannot. You walk into the sea, only to discover that you do not need to breathe. You throw yourself from a cliff, but the rocks below only cause pain, not death. You run yourself through with a sharpened tree branch, but the wound closes and heals without ill effect. Angry and dejected, you leave your island home to find another. Imagine what it must be like to bitterly conclude that you cannot die because you were never alive to begin with; to decide that a beating heart is no great loss. Imagine all that, and maybe you can have a better understanding of what drives someone to wish so much ill on the world around her. Because now, for her, there is only pain. -Memories of Luna, Volume 1, by Roger Ellis

Arrival

"She's out there, somewhere."

Ben didn't know if the statement was true, or who it was referring to. His mind was a swamp of memories, ghost stories, stoic hope, quiet desperation, and every emotion in the spectrum, long ago buried but apparently not quite forgotten—the deepest of which was fear. But fear, like all the other feelings, had seethed its way back up to the surface of his consciousness like a snake that had been living inside the walls of his psyche, and it was ready for a meal. Tonight, however, fear was a luxury he couldn't afford, and it would have to wait its turn. It was hope that would keep his will going until morning, and anger that would move his muscles. Fear was useless, and, for now at least, had to stay buried, no matter how intimidating the landscape in front of him appeared to be.

There was an island ahead. From where he sat in his boat on the water, Ben pondered how much of its ominousness it owed to its appearance, and how much it owed to legend. Once he divorced the land from the myth, he found that there wasn't really anything about the geography itself that suggested outright danger; it was the island's reputation that was setting his senses on edge. The sun was a candle near the end of its wick, the dying light yearning to comfort, but threatening instead. The horizon, by hiding it, would calmly melt away his confident visage and reveal his immediate future for what it actually was—lonely, dark, and frightening. Looking at that island demanded certainty—not doubt—and he was forced to think about his reason for being on the open water, headed toward an unfamiliar shore, determined to find someone who only existed according to local myth. He knew that that reason was about to be the only solid thing in his life. He wrenched his thoughts back to the matter at hand. *She's out there, somewhere,* he thought to himself. He tried again, in vain, to sort out which image those four words invoked in his mind. He couldn't decide. Victim or kidnapper? Damsel or dragon? Angel or devil? What difference did it make? They were in the same place. The words just felt good to say.

He stood up in the little motor boat that had taken him, along with the only friend he had left, to the supposedly uninhabited island that was the subject of countless wives' tales and whispered rumors, taking in the jagged silhouette that seemed to increase its sharpness against the purple and red sky as he stared. As the boat got closer, his apprehension increased with each beat of his heart. He suppressed the urge to swallow, and stuffed his anxiety back down into whatever box it had sprung out of. *Not tonight,* he told himself, *there's just no room for it tonight.*

"Well, it looks quiet, at least," Chris said. Ben had to admit that he agreed. From that side of the island it looked as if most of it was covered in dense forest, with only a few patches here and there near the edges that appeared bare. While Ben didn't relish the idea of running around in such thick greenery all night, the more obvious problem at the moment was reaching said greenery in the first place. The beach they were approaching was stopped shortly up the shore by a sheer rock wall at least two hundred feet high. It kept whatever life was on that island there by wrapping around it as far as either of the adventurers could see and threatening with a fatal drop into the craggy rocks below should anyone get too close to its edge. The left side of the island was fortified by a huge hill that met the end of the natural wall bluntly and looked far too steep to try and climb; it might as well have been a wall in its own right. From where he was, Ben couldn't see a visible entrance to the island's fortified interior, and chances were that there was none given the reputation of the one he was here to see. The entire scene retold pieces of the stories he had heard before shoving off.

The Solitary One don't take kindly to strangers, he had been warned. *She stays out there on her island and we stay off it. Don't nobody here wanna know what she does out there. As long as she ain't botherin' us, breakin' our hearts or scarin' our children, we get along just fine.*

"Well, it *is* a long shot, anyway," Ben said, voicing what was more of a concern for him than a wish. "It's probably uninhabited."

"You *hope,*" said Chris, cracking a wry smile, but not taking his eyes off the cliff.

"No, I don't," corrected Ben. He appreciated his friend's ill-timed humor, but he didn't have it in him to joke. "I didn't come all the way out here to find nothing, even if it *is* what I expect."

"Well the Lunians seem convinced," Chris said. "So what are you going to do if it's true? Do you really want to know what's going on in there?"

Ben stared at his friend a moment, trying to figure out if he had just been asked a trick question. "Of course I do," he said plainly.

Chris simply nodded lightly and continued to squint at the cliff.

Ben cut the motor and was left with the gentle sound of waves lapping against the side of the boat. He knew better than to advertise his arrival. The boat continued on at a crawl, and the closer momentum carried them to the beach the more ominous the island looked and the closer he felt he was to something extraordinary. Still a few hundred feet out, he took another look at the stone wall that at first glance seemed impenetrable, scanning its surface from beach to crest, hoping to see some hint of a possible point of entry. What he saw instead, out of the corner of his vision when his eyes reached the top, was a silhouette against the crimson skyline that hadn't been there a few moments ago. He snapped his head toward it and squinted, feeling his heartbeat quicken as he did so. It was unmistakably human, and it was unmistakably female. The breeze was catching long locks of hair and pushing them toward the sea, and a skirt of some kind whipped and wrapped around slender legs that stood in a pose that was made defiant by the way her arms were held at her sides.

"There's someone there," Ben said softly, not sure whether or not to believe what he was saying. After a moment his eyes widened and he said again with more conviction, "There's someone there." It was obvious that they had been seen, so he no longer felt the need for subtlety. *"Hey!"* He shouted up at the silhouette. *"Hey!"* Just as suddenly as it had caught his attention the shadow vanished behind the crest of the wall, leaving him excited and bewildered at the same time. Like a man possessed he jumped into the water and swam until his feet found something to plant on and trudged onto the beach as quickly as the sea would allow. Chris's shouts of discouragement had been reduced to incoherent mutterings by the chaotic splashing of water in his ears, and his sense of urgency didn't let him notice how cold the warm breeze made his wet clothes as he ran up to the natural wall and searched frantically for footholds. He had come prepared to get dirty, and denim shorts and olive drab-colored tee shirts were good for that kind of thing. When he again found nothing, he backpedaled away from the wall and craned his neck, trying to see as far over the top of the wall as possible, not acknowledging that those efforts were pointless, and shouting at the silhouette that may or may not have even been within earshot anymore. For a split second he had reconsidered making so much racket, but then it occurred to him that there could only be one reason for anyone to come here and that he didn't have anything to hide. The swirling breeze carried his voice in all directions as he demanded the answer to the question that he had come to ask. *"Where is she?!"* Silence was the only answer he was afforded, and Ben felt his wonderings solidify into certainties. *"Please!"* He shouted, his voice lost in a warm, sudden gust of wind that swept down the wall and out toward the sea. *She's out there,* he thought again, still staring up at the crest of the wall as though the island dweller might reappear. *And now she's waiting for me.*

The Vanishing

Ben and Lindsey got off the plane without the sense of being on a business trip. The balmy air and their tourist-like payload of luggage made it seem too much like a vacation, and the immediately noticeable absence of tall buildings and city-like bustle added to the effect. There were docks on both sides of the place where their small airplane had landed in the water, and numerous people fishing on all of them. It was a town that technology hadn't found yet. The sky and the water were both their respective shades of blue, and the air didn't have that urban, carbon-monoxide-infested scent to it that people from cities never noticed anymore because they had forgotten what clean air was like. There were more structures made out of wood than concrete, and aside from the quaint little airport, Ben couldn't see anything that resembled modern living. He felt as though his own day and time had fallen out from under him and dropped him into a time and place which had somehow managed to hide in their own small corner of the world, unnoticed by the natural progression of nature and the ever-more demanding laws of society. At first glance, it was a paradise.

The natives were dark-skinned, friendly people, several of whom insisted on helping the young couple carry their luggage to their hut, a march of just over a mile. They walked with a laid-back gait, the kind that denied the existence of anything urgent, and their clothing was so wildly uncoordinated that Ben had to assume that chaos must have been declared the uniform of the day before his arrival. There was a lot of denim, most of it torn and/or frayed, being worn for shorts (he didn't see trousers on anyone), and everyone was either walking barefoot or wearing sandals. It was the shirts they wore, however, that made them look to Ben and Lindsey like they must have had one massive pile of them somewhere in the village, and they had all taken something to wear while blindfolded at the start of the day. Ben thought he could see every color in the spectrum. Be that as it may, the variety seemed to fit the easy-going, loose-fitting style that the people had chosen as their own.

The walk spanned almost the entire length of the village, which Ben saw functioned mainly on one stretch of dirt road that appeared to be the spine of the close-knit community. The community itself was isolated, being bordered on the right by meadows which gave way in the distance to a small chain of mountains, and beyond that, after a ninety minute drive, was civilization. On the left of the stretch there was only water after a couple hundred feet, and that didn't give way to anything that Ben could see. The aligned arrangement of the huts reminded him a little of a hotel hallway, only here the rooms were more randomly placed and the hallway stretched for a mile. It would be one of the warmest, most cordial miles he had ever walked. Everyone smiled and waved, acknowledging him and Lindsey as though they were old friends who were just returning from a long trip.

They started up the dusty path side by side, both dragging the bags they had been allowed to carry on the outside of the small formation so they could hold hands during the walk. Ben looked at the way wisps of his wife's sandy-blonde hair escaped from her ponytail and went crazy in the wind, and was reminded of the day he had proposed. She had had almost exactly the same look to her those three years ago. Ponytail disarrayed by the strong breeze—she had never liked using hair products—blue jeans and a sweater that matched the season, and icy-blue eyes that had never reflected anything but warmth. Lindsey had always loved the outdoors, and until Ben had met her, rock climbing had only been something he had seen in military commercials. He smiled when he thought about how much she had brought into his life, and as always, she was quick to notice and return the gesture.

"What is it?" She asked with the sly, playful curiosity of someone who felt that they were about to be the butt of an inside joke.

"Nothing," came the answer. "I'm just glad you could come." Lindsey leaned over and pecked him on the cheek.

"Me too," she said, still smiling. The rest of the walk made Ben feel like they were dating again. They had nowhere pressing to be, and no one was waiting for them at their destination. It was just them, alone with the world and its beauty, for the moment. No more conversation was made for most of the walk. Ben was content with having time to be with his wife, and Lindsey seemed to be enjoying the atmosphere that was created by the friendly people, the weather, and time away from her daily life. A little over ten minutes into the stroll, one of the villagers pointed to one of the huts (it was impossible to tell which) near the end of the path about a quarter mile ahead.

Lindsey's eyes lit up suddenly and she said, "Race you to the hut!" She dashed forward before she had even finished her sentence, past the locals and down the path, her wheeled duffel bag skipping and sliding close behind her. Ben, never having been one to refuse a challenge, did his best to close the distance over the last quarter mile but didn't catch her until they reached the door of the hut. After using the wall of what they correctly guessed was their temporary new home to stop themselves at the end of the heat, they both leaned over, hands on knees, panting furiously.

Ben looked up between gasps and grinned. "Good thing you had a head start," he commented.

"Yeah—that wasn't fair," came the retort. "That's why I never really floored it."

The rest of their baggage finished the hike at the same slow, laid-back pace at which everything in the village moved. Once their heart rates had returned to normal, the natives had caught up. They were approached by the tallest of the group, a forty-or-so looking man with friendly eyes, a huge, bright smile, and the trademark tropical accent that was part of what made the locals and their town so intriguing. There was nothing about his wardrobe that distinguished him from the other natives, but something about the way he carried himself—with a bit more purpose, perhaps—immediately made it apparent that if they had a spokesman, he was it. He came forward and extended a hand toward Ben.

"Ben Teagan," he said with a rich, colorful voice that suggested that English might have been a second language. "Welcome to our town of Luna. Natives and visitors alike call me Roger." Ben instantly recognized the name.

"You're the man I'm here to see?" The surprise in Ben's voice only made Roger's smile wider. "Why didn't you say something earlier?"

"I wanted you to get a taste of our paradise before I approached you with business," Roger explained. "We have a nice little slice of Heaven here, would you agree?"

"From what I've seen so far, I would say so," Ben admitted in the friendliest business tone he knew.

"There will be time for the full tour later," Roger said. "For now, why don't you and your wife make yourselves at home? In a few hours, after the sun goes down, there will be a gathering out here on the main stretch; our humble version of the better-known Hawaiian luau. The two of you should come out then and we can talk more. Is it a date?" Even if Ben hadn't wanted to go, the man's personality made the request impossible to refuse.

"It certainly is," he said with closed eyes, a slight bow, and a friendly smile. Roger returned the gesture almost reflexively.

"Then I hope you like to eat fish," he said, and with a flourish and a turn he led his group of locals away from their guests, leaving the two of them alone.

Ben pushed the door of the hut open and gestured for Lindsey to enter with a slow, sweeping motion. "After you, my lady," he announced chivalrously. Lindsey moved past him, tousling his short, brown hair as she went by.

"What a gentleman I married," she cooed. Ben dragged his bag in behind her and closed the door. Lindsey laid her bag in front of the pile that the locals had made in the corner with the rest of her luggage and flopped down on the queen-sized bed that was 95 percent of the room's furnishing. She took a minute to admire the simplicity of the room—the windows that were nothing more than frames in the wall, the square footage that allowed for a two person bed and not much more—and sighed. "This place is so... inviting, so apart from everything else. I think people are really going to like coming here. Who wouldn't love a week in paradise?"

"If this was really paradise," Ben pointed out, "why would the natives want to change it, or share it for that matter? Although I have to admit that the quaint welcome was a nice sales pitch."

"Always business, huh?" Lindsey said chidingly.

"That *is* why I'm here," he answered, smiling wryly.

"I swear, I'm going to get you to relax down here if it's the last thing I do." Ben's grin became a full smile at the running gag. One of the biggest differences between him and his wife had always been rigidity. It was one of the few aspects of his personality that Lindsey hadn't yet had some kind of effect on.

"Don't hold your breath," he warned. He didn't say that because he meant it anymore. He only said it because it was what he had always said.

"Believe me, I'm not," came the reply, resigned but loving. Lindsey rolled off the bed and went into the tiny bathroom, which was the only other room in the hut. "It looks like they have plumbing."

"If they plan on attracting tourists, they'd better," Ben said. "People will only want to experience their way of life to a certain degree. If they lose comfort, they lose interest."

Lindsey came out of the bathroom and sat on the edge of the bed. "Speaking of comfort... and interest..." she trailed off and patted the bed next to where she was sitting, tilting her head at an angle that made sure her message got through. Ben sat next to his wife and put his arm around her.

"I love you," he said. Lindsey always knew what to say in response.

"I love you, too."

The sounds of laughter and broken conversation called them out hours later. When they walked out onto the main stretch they were met with nighttime, the dim glow of firelight, and the scent of cooked meat. The locals had built a bonfire on the path and seemed to be enjoying the day's catch with all the merriment. Hand in hand, Ben and Lindsey approached the crowd, watching some of the more young and agile ones dart around like fireflies in the glow of the blaze. Ben saw Roger sitting in a folding chair near the outside of the hub of commotion (but just inside enough so as not to seem lofty or inaccessible to the other villagers) and eating a freshly-cooked fish with his bare hands. When they made eye contact through the buzz of activity, Roger waved them over to the two empty chairs across from him that he had presumably been saving for them.

"It's good to see you love birds out and about," he greeted without getting up, making the encounter seem that much more friendly and informal. "Would you care for some fish?"

"No, thanks;" Ben said as he took a seat, "I'm good right now." Roger then looked at Lindsey, whose stomach wasn't as patient.

"I would love some," she said, "any kind you have over there would be fine." Roger waved to get the attention of a child racing around the fire with friends and motioned for some fish to be brought.

"So what exactly are you looking to accomplish here, Roger?" Ben asked. "In the big picture, I mean."

"Straight to the point!" Roger observed happily, "I knew I contacted the right people. As you know, I have a mind to see this place realize its full potential. I think it's time that Luna was introduced to the rest of the world, or rather, the world was introduced to Luna. If people could see on a large scale what kind of place this can be, we could really have something on our hands."

"Something?" Lindsey interjected.

"A higher standard of living, for one thing," Roger explained. "Opportunities for our young ones, for another."

"I thought that the standard of living here was supposed to be part of the appeal," Ben said. "If you raise it, what would separate Luna from a place like Hawaii?"

"Even if we improve our lives here we should be able to maintain the primitive illusions for the sake of the tourists," Roger argued. "Not to mention the spirit of competition. Hawaii is an expensive vacation, is it not? *Everyone* will be able to come and spend a week in Luna. Consider, this is not an island, and if inexpensive transportation could be arranged from the city, at our own expense of course, that would be a good start toward keeping the cost down for the average tourist."

"That's good in theory," Ben pointed out, "but this place doesn't really seem big enough to make it affordable for *everyone*. Aren't you concerned about overbooking?"

"There are capacity issues, true," Roger admitted, "but over the long run I think our town would benefit more from the bankable income on a waiting list than it would from catering only to the superbly wealthy; nothing says we have to overbook, and with the proper plan, the limited space will only help to increase demand. And who knows? Maybe someday, if we are successful enough, then there may come a time to adjust our clientele."

Ben gave it a slow, thoughtful nod. "And can I assume that at least part of the money you need from me is for staffing, then?"

Roger showed a smile, so brilliant it was startling, before he answered, scooting to the edge of his chair. "That is the true beauty of our model," he explained. "The staff is already here, and will work for free!"

Ben looked around at the festivities. "You've convinced the entire town to work for free, toward an end that will probably change their entire way of life?" He asked dubiously.

"Luna is an old place, Ben," Roger said. "We mostly self-sustain. And if our model is successful, all we need them to do is keep doing what they already do: live an authentic Lunian lifestyle. I don't envision a new town full of amusement park rides and carnival games; I envision a true paradise, more authentic than people from your world would expect. I believe people would relish the chance to live like us for a week or two, provided they feel safe and comfortable doing it." Roger studied Ben's face for a moment, and continued. "There are many details that need to be ironed out yet, I know. We will need infrastructure, transportation, and marketing, among other things, but I remain optimistic. For now, let it simply be said that I have a plan, and my people trust me."

"You certainly do," Ben assessed, nodding. "This is quite an undertaking you have planned here, isn't it?"

"It *will* take time and dedication," Roger admitted. Then, looking at Ben squarely, he added the obvious, "And funding." Roger's suddenly-serious tone made Ben chuckle a bit.

"Yes, well, what doesn't?" He asked rhetorically.

"Indeed," Roger said.

"I'll tell you what," Ben suggested. "Give us a day or two to look over things here, maybe make our rounds and talk to some of the locals, and we'll go over this thing with a fine-toothed comb."

Roger's smile was as warm as the bonfire. "By all means, take all the time you need. We have waited so long as it is, what are another few days? Besides," he added, "here in Luna we do not like to rush."

"I can tell," Ben said appreciatively. "Just the same, we won't take any longer than we need to."

Roger smiled gratefully. "Then I look forward to speaking again soon," he said.

"We will," Ben said. "Right now I think I'm about ready to nod off." He looked over at Lindsey and patted her knee. "You ready?" Lindsey's responsive yawn ended in a tired-looking smile.

"I think so," she answered. "Thanks for the fish." Roger waved her gratitude off as something completely unnecessary.

"You two sleep well, and enjoy your time here," Roger said, this time rising with them as they prepared to leave. "If there is anything you need in the meantime, you can find me at my house, just off the end of the stretch on the left." He pointed down the path in the direction he was speaking. The two nodded, thanked him again with a wave, and started back up the "stretch" toward their hut.

"It's a shame they want to turn this place into a tourist attraction," Lindsey said once they were away from the crowd. "There are a lot of people in other parts of the world who would give anything to have their lives revert back to…this."

"I guess the grass is always greener on the other side, and all that jazz," Ben responded.

"Yeah," Lindsey said with a hint of disappointment, "but it's still a shame."

It didn't take long for either of them to fall asleep once they were back inside and on the surprisingly comfortable bed. "I'll give Roger one thing," Ben said as he drifted off, "he knows what people on vacation need."

"I didn't think we were on vacation," Lindsey teased. Ben laughed as he rolled over and hugged his wife.

"Neither did I."

"Good night, Sugar."

"Good night." They could still barely hear the crackling of the huge fire outside on the path as their consciousness was stolen by the balmy air and soft moonlight drifting in through a window. *If this is a typical night in Luna,* Ben thought, *changing it* would *be a shame.* In the next few moments, he was asleep.

In what seemed like the *next* few moments, he was awake again. At first he was caught in that stage of half-sleep in which things were perceived, but dreaming was still possible. A very short amount of time passed, however, before it registered in his mind that there was something out of place. Instinctively he reached over to find Lindsey, but was only met with sheets that were no longer even warm. Ben immediately opened his eyes fully, not assuming anything terrible but still wanting to get a handle on where his wife had gone. She might have been feeling sick—who knew what kind of fish she had eaten earlier? Neither of them had bothered to ask. Or maybe she had enjoyed the atmosphere enough that she decided to take a stroll out on the path while the night was still so intimate. She did things like that sometimes, but it was strange that she hadn't woken him to tell him where she would be. He propped himself up with one arm and looked around at everything that the moonlight would let him see. There was no sound outside now save for the occasional chirping of crickets and the distant crashing of waves on a beach. The fire had gone out and the villagers had gone to their own homes to sleep. It felt to him like the time must have been somewhere between two and three in the morning. Ben spoke loudly enough so that Lindsey could have heard him if she had been in the bathroom, but low enough so as not to wake the neighbors.

"Lindsey?" No answer. "Are you okay in there?" Still no answer. He rolled out of bed and went outside to look down the path. It was a full moon night, there was nothing obstructing the view, and still Lindsey was nowhere to be seen. He went around to the side of the hut that sat away from the path, hoping that she had decided to sit there and stargaze, but still he found everything except what he was looking for. Ben's face was a portrait of confusion and concern as he called out, loudly this time, "Lindsey?" His pace quickened and he went back around to the front of the hut, calling louder still, "Lindsey!"

"How is everything? Okay?" Ben hadn't noticed one of the lighter sleeping villagers come out of the neighboring hut to see what the commotion was about. Normally he would have been apologetic, but this time his apology was only a formality.

"I'm sorry I woke you. Have you seen my wife?" Ben asked the question knowing that a sleeping man would probably not have seen anything, but he found himself willing to roll the dice. He was running down the stretch before the man even had time to shake his head in response. Even running at a strong pace, Ben didn't so much as feel the mile between himself and the end of it. When he got there, there was still no sign of Lindsey, and he immediately started running back up the way he came, now shouting as loudly as sprinting would allow, no longer caring about who he woke up or how foolish he would look if she had just gone somewhere he had yet to check. *"Lindsey! Lindsey!"* People were peering out of windows and doors as he ran, beside himself with worry, back up the path toward his hut. Halfway there he remembered Roger and instantly doubled back once again, this time looking for help from the only man in Luna who seemed to even resemble an authority figure. As he thought about it, Ben wondered if they even *had* police in Luna. When he again reached the end of the stretch and looked for Roger's house, he was thankful that it stood out. It was a bit farther off the path than the rest of the tiny community and it was actually a *house.* He sprinted up to the porch and pounded on the front door. *"Roger? Are you home?"*

Roger was downstairs and at the door as though he drilled for these occasions in his spare time and began trying to calm down the frantic city fellow who was too excited to explain himself. In his sky blue bathrobe he looked every bit to Ben like a low-budget tropical gigolo. "Easy now, easy Ben, what is the problem?"

"Lindsey's gone," he said, panting furiously and leaning against the door frame for support. "I've looked all up and down this stretch of road and she's nowhere." Even in his panicked state, Ben appreciated the instant, and genuine, look of concern on Roger's face.

"Did you try the beach and docks near the airport?" Roger asked.

Ben shook his head. "I haven't gotten that far yet. Hopefully she's down there, but I think she would have heard me by now if she was."

Roger nodded. "Go check. I will call the police." Ben was off the porch and running toward the beach before Roger had finished his sentence. "Give them time!" He shouted. "They have to come from the city!" Ben didn't care if they had to come from Bangkok.

He didn't stop sprinting until he was standing on one of the fishing docks near the airport. He looked around at the beach and saw that he was still alone. As his eyes welled up with fear and frustration, he felt himself getting angry with his wife. She had to be somewhere close. How could she leave in the dead of night for some unknown place and not at least tell him where she was going, or just *that* she was going? No wife should scare a husband like that. But what if it was something else? What if she had slipped on a rock and was knocked out? In a place like this, it would be easy to get carried off by waves if one lost consciousness in the wrong place and at the wrong time.

The breeze was stronger coming in off of the water and it felt too much like loneliness; Ben had to turn his face away from it and ignore everything for a few minutes. He had to ignore the crashing waves and all their suggestions and stories of eternal cycling, had to ignore the stars and their sudden insistence that eventually all things must end, and most of all he had to ignore the wind and its relentless scolding of his efforts to not go through life alone. *There's no need to think like this,* he admonished himself. *Don't be so melodramatic. It's only been twenty minutes and there are plenty of places still to check.* No amount of sense, however, was able to suppress that gut feeling that there was something out of place. It took him a few minutes to start on his way back because something (maybe instinct, *hopefully* paranoia) told him to come to grips with the worst case scenario before he went back up the stretch and started answering inevitable questions that he didn't want to be asked. *So what's the worst case scenario? She might never be found, she might be found dead, or you might get a letter two weeks from now from an anonymous place that says she's tired of dealing with you and screw off. Better start dealing with that now.* Not entirely sold on the necessity of such self-abuse, Ben opted instead to hope for the best. *She's just in a place no one has looked. We'll find her napping under the stars somewhere and she'll wonder what all the fuss was about.* It made the trek back to the stretch easier.

The trademark red and blue lights of police cars spinning and announcing their presence on every flat surface in the area was one of the most unwelcome sights Ben had ever had the displeasure of laying eyes on. It made the recently paradise-like village look too much like a crime scene, and it plunged his thoughts into a downward spiral of fear and despair. The situation wasn't helped by the villagers, most of whom were now awake and inquisitive, standing around in small mobs and talking in low voices about things that Ben wasn't interested in hearing yet.

Oh my God, she's dead. They found her dead.

Ben was in no hurry to hear the news that he knew was coming, and finished the hike at the same clip at which he had started it. From the outside he looked like a man who was more dejected and indecisive than concerned. When Roger looked up and saw that his search of the docks had yielded nothing, he waved Ben over to where he was standing with an officer who was clearly not local.

"Mr. Teagan?" He said. Ben looked at the nametag on the officer's shirt and read "Mathis." He nodded, unable to speak. "When was the last time you saw your wife, Sir?"

Ben's heart felt as though it was about to tear itself in half. "...You haven't found her yet?" He asked tentatively. It came as a huge relief to Ben, who had thought that he would be identifying a body, but Mathis misinterpreted the question as impatience.

"No, Sir, but a search *is* underway. You need to keep in mind that this may not resolve itself for a very undesirable amount of time. It's best that you prepare for that."

"No, I understand," Ben assured, not feeling it necessary to smooth out the misunderstanding. "And thank you for coming as quickly as you did. Roger told me to expect a bit of a wait." Indeed, the troopers had shown up on the scene with a punctuality he would have thought impossible considering the town's location, but Ben had been too grateful to be alarmed.

"Well, this certainly isn't the first instance of something like this here," said Mathis. "We have people who have been trying to get to the bottom of this thing for a long time. How long ago did your wife disappear?" Out of the corner of his eye, Ben saw Roger close his eyes and clench his teeth. He blinked a few times before answering, needing to let the revelation sink in before he could shake the surprise off and be cooperative.

"I'm not sure, really," he said. "We fell asleep together in our hut and when I woke up she was just... gone."

"You didn't hear anything? Didn't see anyone enter or leave?"

"No, I didn't even feel it when she got out of bed," Ben admitted, still mystified as to how he could have possibly been sleeping *that* soundly. The officer nodded as though it was something he was used to hearing.

"And how long have you been awake?"

"About an hour now, I guess," Ben said. His mind was still stuck a few moments in the past. "This is a recurring problem?"

"Unfortunately so," said Mathis. "Every once in a while there's a case of a disappearance here, but this is the first time an out-of-towner has ever been involved."

"Every once in a while?" Ben echoed. "How often?"

"Every few years, I'd say," Mathis said. "But this time we know a little more than we have in the past... sort of. We've been keeping the roads under surveillance since the last incident, and Luna's off-road terrain doesn't really allow for vehicles to get to the town any other way. Whoever is doing this is on foot, but we have no idea where they're coming from or how they're leaving town."

"You're assuming Lindsey was kidnapped?" Ben asked.

"Yes, I am," Mathis said bluntly. "Like I said, this isn't the first occurrence here. Naturally, we'll conduct a search of the shore in case, God forbid, your wife was simply involved in an accident of some kind, but I find it highly unlikely given the short amount of time she's been missing and still not found."

"What if they're *not* leaving town?" Ben suggested, desperately needing a reason to believe that death wasn't the case. A kidnapping would be bad, but at least it might have a palatable conclusion.

"Mr. Teagan, this place has been combed many times in the past for this exact reason. We've never found a place to hide cargo like that."

Ben spoke again when he thought he had wrapped his head around what he was being told. "So you're telling me that someone came into this village on foot, *silently* stole my wife out of our bed while we were sleeping, and disappeared with her somewhere along the countryside without being seen or heard by *anyone?"* Ben's doubtful tone didn't faze the veteran officer.

"Actually, Mr. Teagan, that's what *you* seem to be telling *me."* Ben looked around at the scene surrounding him. Groups of natives were being systematically questioned by policemen who seemed to be used to the lack of information they were obviously getting. The village was a circus of shrugs and heads shaking, glances down the stretch, and random chatter.

"No one saw *anything?*" He asked hopelessly.

"Not so far," Mathis said, "and if history is any indication, I wouldn't expect much."

Ben nodded, his eyes once again welling up with tears. "Well," he said sincerely, "I'm glad the situation has warranted so much attention. I'm really glad to see that you guys brought so many people out here."

"It's no trouble at all, Sir," said Mathis sympathetically. "We want to put a stop to this as much as anyone." Ben nodded again and extended his hand, and Mathis shook it firmly.

"Thanks," he said. "If you guys need to get a hold of me, find Roger." Mathis nodded in response.

"Keep your head up," said Mathis. "We'll find her." Ben smiled half-heartedly and started walking away from the center of activity, thinking it was probably best to find a seat and try to sort something—anything—out. As he walked through the broken crowds of bystanders and inquisitors he noticed that voices grew more hushed as he passed. The already indiscernible pieces of chatter made by the locals became even quieter when he got close, as if they didn't want to mention the obvious within hearing distance of the victim. Ben stopped walking, frowned, and shook his head lightly at nothing in particular. He couldn't make anything add up. He looked around at the scattered crowd and took in what he saw. A few locals pointing up the road and shaking their heads, officers writing on pads of paper with stone faces and nodding solemnly, all the randomly placed people made psychedelic by the rotating lights of the police cruisers. A few of the officers were holding their cell phones to the sky, trying to find a signal. The exercise in futility struck Ben as both humorous and strangely unprofessional. His mind briefly touched on the observation that there were almost *too many* officers on the scene, but a group of locals caught his eye before he gave it any thought. A few of the natives were standing apart from the rest of the activity and he was instantly curious. Having already been questioned, they weren't paying much attention to anything other than the water, regarding it with a serenity that was clearly unique to the situation. Ben started walking toward them, but when they noticed that he was coming the group disbanded; not urgently, but in a manner that suggested they didn't want to attract attention. Ben quickened his pace to reach them before they spread out too far and addressed the first one he reached.

"What's out there?" He asked curiously.

The old man looked at him squarely with sad eyes and replied in the emptiest tone Ben had ever heard. "Just water," he said. The others in the group were watching the interaction with guarded interest and Ben felt the need to press further.

"Why are we staring at it?" The man simply continued to stare at him with that same guarded sadness, and Ben was sure that there was something he wasn't being told although he couldn't begin to guess the motive for withholding information at a time like this. He was in no mood to beat around the bush or be jerked around, and he was about to tell the man so when Roger put a hand on his shoulder.

"There you are," he said. "I was worried that you had gone off on your own again."

Ben was now impervious to anyone's concern. "Roger, there's something I'm not being told. What is it?" Roger diverted his eyes to the old man, who simply turned and started walking away.

"This is not an issue that should be pressed, Ben," he advised. "Micah keeps to himself for a reason."

"I don't doubt that," Ben said, "I just want to be sure that that reason doesn't have anything to do with my wife."

"I assure you that it does not," said Roger. "It has something to do with *his.*" Ben stared blankly at Roger until he explained. "Years ago Micah's wife was lost to the sea." He inclined his head in the direction that the small group had minutes ago been looking. "She drowned not far off the beach. I would guess that someone else missing a wife is reminding him of how badly he misses his." Ben looked around for Micah, feeling guilty and wanting to apologize, but he was nowhere to be seen. Roger read his expression easily. "I'm sure he understands how frantic you are," he consoled. "Micah is not the begrudging kind." Ben was happy to turn his thoughts to other places.

"I can't believe no one saw anything," he said, feeling exasperated. "Why do they only watch the road? What would stop someone from coming here by boat?"

"The rocks out there do not allow it," Roger said. "The water is not as deep as it seems until you get almost a mile out."

"Then she must still be *here,*" Ben said, all over again losing patience with the mystery.

"There is no place here to hide a person," Roger insisted, speaking gently to avoid a confrontation, the way a parent spoke to a child who was prone to tantrums. "The police have searched many times. If there was a place, they would have found it by now."

"Unless the ones searching are the ones taking," Ben rationalized bitterly.

"Easy now," said Roger, motioning lightly toward Ben as if trying to stop traffic. "A town as small as this one has no choice but to trust people outside of it for some things. Their concern seems genuine enough to me."

"How many times has this happened here?" Ben wanted to know. "The officer over there told me that this wasn't the first." Roger looked at the ground and nodded, giving Ben the feeling that he would rather not have been asked.

"Twenty-seven," he said quietly. "It has been four years since the last one."

"Twenty-seven?!" Ben repeated, not bothering to mimic Roger's discreet tone of voice. After a pause he asked, "How many years since the *first* one?"

"We are not sure," Roger answered. "These crimes predate us all."

"This has been going on *that long?"* Ben exclaimed, stunned by the revelation and vagueness of the statistics. "And it hasn't been stopped yet?"

"The police say that there is no pattern," Roger said defensively. "They say that there is no possible way to come in without being seen or to leave without getting caught, that there is no readily apparent motive, and that whoever does it must hold a terrible grudge and be at least a *fourth generation* offender. Who keeps this up for such a long time? And despite all this, we have found nothing. Many times the police have tried to figure out what the victims have in common, and until now the only answer was that they all came from the same place. So much for that." By the time Roger had finished speaking Ben's eyes had welled up again.

"You're telling me that Lindsey will never be found," he said, his voice weak and hopeless.

"Certainly not," Roger said sternly. "You keep your head up, Ben, and this thing will fall into place." When he saw that his words were beginning to fall on distant ears he put his arm around Ben and led him away from the center of activity and onto his front porch where he sat him on a wooden bench that let him look out toward the crowd. "I am going to go tell the police where to find you if they need you, and I will be back with some coffee." He patted Ben on the shoulder and headed back out to the commotion, leaving Ben to come to grips with things on his own terms.

The minutes that passed seemed like hours, each one lengthened by the fear that at any moment he would be approached by one of the officers and told that his wife had finally been found, only not quite in the condition that he remembered. Roger came and went, checking on him periodically to make sure that he was comfortable and that his spirits were as high as they could be. After a few hours Ben saw that the people were finally starting to go back to their homes, all the gossip having been exchanged and a good night's sleep interrupted. More cruisers had been showing up as well, and even though Ben could have sworn that the officer driving each one would deliver the news that had terrified him throughout the night, that news never came. Roger kept him updated each time he returned to the porch, and every officer had the same thing to report. Nothing had been seen, no one had been found, no one knew what the hell was going on in Luna. All he could do was watch helplessly as people moved back and forth, and unknowingly witness the one night of his life that

31

would be remembered over all others for years to come. It was approaching dawn by the time the last of the patrollers returned with his findings, and Ben was still on Roger's porch fighting a losing battle with his tears when Mathis came to see him.

"I assume Roger has been keeping you up to speed about what's going on," Mathis began. Ben nodded, looking at the officer through tired eyes that could have closed and stayed closed for a full day if only his wrenched heart would have let them. "Our guys weren't able to find anything," he confirmed. Ben nodded again, not surprised but still stung by the way that the spoken words made his hope dwindle. "As soon as we find something out, Mr. Teagan, you'll be the first to know." Ben nodded again and spoke without hearing his own words.

"Thanks for all your time," he said hoarsely. Mathis smiled encouragingly and nodded, then turned and went down the steps and back to his own cruiser. A few moments later, the only signs of anything out of place at all in Luna were two men sitting on a porch just off the stretch, one doing his best to console the other, whose head hurt from worrying but was still unable to rest. Half of the sun was visible before either one of them spoke.

"Is there anything I can do?" Roger asked solemnly. It was a long time before Ben answered.

"I don't even know what *I'm* going to do," he said softly.

"I am truly sorry that I cannot do more," Roger said. Hearing sympathy made Ben's voice leave him as he replied, shaking his head.

"It's okay." It was mid-morning before Ben fell asleep on Roger's bench, his exhaustion finally outweighing his pain.

Leaving Luna without his wife had been the single hardest thing Ben had ever had to make himself do. He stalled for a few days, not willing to relinquish the hope that part of him still clung on to. But with each passing hour, reality had become more undeniable. He knew that the world wasn't going to wait for him simply because of misfortune. There was still business to attend to, and he had already put it all on hold for the four extra days that he had stayed in Luna. On the afternoon of that fourth day, he had made himself start going through the motions. Going back into the hut for the first time since Lindsey's disappearance hadn't been enjoyable. The bed sheets were still just as he had left them when he had rolled out of bed and onto the stretch, and packing Lindsey's things had been no picnic, either. It was surprising how many things that reminded him of that night could be crammed into a room as small as the one that they had slept in, but somehow the tiny hut had managed to house a hundred painful memories that were all there to greet Ben when he went back for their luggage. The departure had been an emotional nightmare. It had hurt to carry two sets of bags by himself, it had hurt to not have anyone to talk to while he prepared to leave, it had hurt to have to tell a man as friendly and well-meaning as Roger that he would have to find another way to fund his project. Most of all, though, it had hurt to board a plane not knowing whether or not his wife was still alive, or where she was, or if she was bound and gagged in a corner somewhere praying for rescue. Leaving without her had made him feel like an awful husband and an even worse human being, and even though he knew that he had done the only thing he *could* do, he never found a way to forgive himself.

He had gotten on the plane with Roger's promise that if Lindsey ever turned up he would let Ben know. By the time he had resigned himself to leaving, however, Ben had already started to regard words like those as arbitrary and hollow, no matter whom they were coming from. He knew that no one expected to see Lindsey again, and he wished that people would stop making it sound as if there was still hope. Even if Ben had believed that there was, he knew that they didn't.

So he had left Luna miserable, and from that day forward life had more or less stayed that way. He had grown to hate himself for sleeping so soundly and allowing someone to come into his room and steal his wife, and as a result he never had another good night's sleep. Falling asleep was the same drill it had been on that first night in Luna—he was usually only able to fall out when he exhausted himself. It was emotionally draining to continue to live in the same house that he and Lindsey had shared, but he was afraid to sell it on the off chance that she would show up one day. Every foreign sound in every room sounded like a distant knock on the front door, but after a few months he figured out that he was making himself hear half of them and decided to stop answering the door for no one before the situation became unhealthier than it already was. His daily life had continued—business deals, stock trades, and other financial ventures—but with the exceptions of work and his friend Chris, Ben didn't have any contact with the outside world. Each day became more and more like a mechanical kind of survival. Motions were repeated and things were accomplished, but life itself seemed to have nothing more to offer. Ben only survived because he was used to it. He had survived the initial disappearance, he had survived the transition back to his home life, and over the first few months he had survived all the accusations that Lindsey's family had thrown at him. He had never bothered acknowledging them because he didn't know what to believe about himself anymore anyway. So much had changed so quickly, and life was simply not what it used to be.

It was on the afternoon of one of those mundanely hollow days that emotions were stirred in Ben that he had no longer believed he was capable of; it had been almost two years since Lindsey went missing and each day had become indiscernible from the last. Checking the mail had become more of a weekly event than a daily one; he had lost interest in what the rest of the world wanted with him. But after one of those weekly trips to the end of his long lane and the mailbox, almost invisible in the accordion-like configuration of credit card offers, political flyers, and coupon books was a letter actually addressed to him. Reading it only seemed like a formality when he saw that the return address was in Luna. The immediate fear of what was on the inside of that envelope froze Ben's heart for a few seconds. He stared at the unopened letter in his hand for a minute; it wasn't readily apparent to him what he should do with it. It had been a long time since he had bothered opening any mail; it had been a long time since anyone had sent him a letter. For a brief few moments he considered not opening it at all; he realized that opening the letter might only confirm the reality of something that he had almost succeeded in burying his fear of. But it wasn't long before he admitted that not knowing what it said couldn't possibly make life any better. He opened it and saw a single sentence centered on a small piece of folded paper:

Your wife is across the water—Roger

Ben read the sentence repeatedly, making sure that there wasn't some other way to take the information, but the bluntness of the message didn't leave much room for misinterpretation. Each time his eyes passed over the words he felt a long lost sense of urgency start to surge inside of him, at first a subtle throbbing at the center of his being but stronger after every reading. It spread from there out to his limbs, and his shoulders and thighs tensed. It crept out to his extremities, and his hands began to tremble with fear and excitement. Tears again blurred his vision, as they had done so often recently, and before long he sprang into action. He dropped all the mail onto the floor and started making phone calls, first to Chris, then to an airline. Chris had left his office immediately and had shown up ready to ship, three piece suit and all, but ultimately the two of them decided it would be best to make sure they had all their ducks lined up (and clothes changed) before taking off. By the time the sun set on the next day the two of them were on a commercial airliner to the closest city to Luna.

The flight was tense for Ben, and neither he nor his friend made much attempt at conversation, although there was a point at which Chris asked him what he expected to find.

"I don't mean to sound pessimistic, Ben," he said. "Lord knows, I hope that we get there and she's waiting for you with bells on and the whole nine, but..."

Ben, whose face had been practically carved out of stone lately, prodded without turning to face his friend. "But?"

"But you've been in pretty bad shape lately, and I don't want you to do anything drastic if this doesn't turn out to be all that you've spent the last twenty-four hours hyping it up to be." Ben saw the sense in preparing for disappointment, especially after Chris reminded him of the reality of time. "It's been *two years.*"

What he said was true, but in Ben's mind there were too many reasons to finally hope for, and maybe even expect, the best. He had felt all along that there had been something withheld from him that night in Luna, although he had no idea what it might have been or who had been holding out. At the moment, "who" figured to be Roger. He didn't care about what the reasons were; that was one of several issues that could be resolved after he had gotten his wife back, if he decided that it was even relevant at that point. Furthermore, why would Roger have even contacted him at all, knowing how distraught the message would make him, if there was nothing to find out there? No—he wasn't going to come away from this trip empty handed; he could feel it.

"I feel good about it," Ben answered simply. "But the message kind of made it sound like we'd have to go get her."

"The fact that she's still alive—if she is—pretty much points to a kidnapping, doesn't it?"

Ben nodded thoughtfully. "I'd say so, yeah."

"What are you going to do if you find her still in captivity? Are you going to try to... you know... exact justice?"

Ben reflected on the last two years of his life, and how that same life had instantly become the single-minded pursuit of his wife the moment that letter had arrived. "I don't need justice," he said solemnly. "I need Lindsey."

As the plane touched down, the two of them worked out the transportation issues. Ben assumed that they would need a boat at some point and left Chris in the city to see to it that they got one. Ben himself found a pilot for hire who was willing to fly the relatively short distance to Luna and touched down there thirty minutes later.

Ben felt his adrenaline begin to rush in anticipation when he again found himself on the docks, but his exterior was calm. He instantly noticed, with little surprise, that the place hadn't changed a bit since he'd last seen it. Despite Roger's efforts to expand and commercialize, he would have a hard time finding sponsors as long as people kept disappearing. It had occurred to him long ago that that had probably been the reason he had neglected to tell Ben about the town's mysterious history in the first place. Once his plane had gone back the way it came, he also noticed the quiet. There was no entourage waiting for him this time as his presence was likely unannounced. There was no reason to sell this time because he wasn't planning on buying anything. There was only the hypnotic sound of waves softly crashing on the beach as he made the short walk from the docks to Roger's house.

He stepped up onto Roger's porch and knocked as amiably as he could. Roger's eyes lit up when he opened his front door and saw Ben, but Ben hadn't been much of a conversationalist.

"Did you find something?" He asked. Roger herded him inside before he could ask too many questions. Once the door was closed behind them he looked Ben over and spoke sympathetically.

"You do not look like you have been getting much sleep, my friend."

"You could say that," Ben said, "but it's slowly getting better. Until your letter came, anyway... she's across what water?" Roger seemed undecided about whether or not he wanted to go through with his explanation, but Ben wasn't going to tolerate any second guessing. "Don't back out on me now," he said with a voice that didn't leave room for argument, "I didn't fly all the way out here for the weather."

Roger took a deep breath before delivering his disclaimer. "Ben, you are going to have to keep an open mind because much of this will be hard to believe. But know that this is something that we in Luna have grown to take as fact, and I have no doubt that it is the source of your troubles."

"Okay, let's have it," Ben said, trying not to sound too impatient. The look on Roger's face as he spoke told him that even if his story was insane, it was serious business to him.

Roger continued in a voice reserved for conversations behind locked doors. "There are stories here of a monster, one that is green with envy, who is responsible for the disappearances of our loved ones. She lives on an island out there in the sea, and there she keeps her victims. I am certain it is where your wife is as well."

"A monster?" Ben said.

Roger closed his eyes and nodded, expecting the incredulity. "People say she had her heart broken some time ago. The one she loved hurt her badly, and now she sees to it that no one stays happy. Jealousy, is all. She cannot find her love, so she just takes other peoples'. Takes them out there to that island, and keeps them there for as long as they live. My brother was married no more than a year before Lornamair came and took his wife away. My old friend and I knew a man married a year; she took her on their anniversary. All because of jealousy. She lives for being jealous, and she *does not die out there.*"

"…Doesn't die?" Ben echoed, not knowing what to think. "How is that possible? What is she?"

"No one here really knows exactly what she is, and when you put things in perspective, no one here cares. We only know that it is she who tries to make our lives miserable by exacting revenge on her unfaithful husband through innocent people who want nothing more than to live safely and in peace. You are but one of many who made the mistake of loving his wife too much in Luna."

"Assuming that what you're saying is true," Ben said, "how does she get here without being seen?"

Roger spread his hands helplessly. "We don't know."

Ben turned things over in his head for a minute. "This *is* hard to believe."

"All the same," said Roger, "If you find Lornamair, I promise that you will also find your wife."

"Why did it take two years to tell me this?"

"Because to go out there is suicide," Roger said. "No one has ever seen the old witch and lived to tell about it. There have been those of us who tried to take back what she stole, but we never saw them again. I could not in good conscience send a man to die out there, especially one who did not realize what he would be up against. But after so much time went by I decided that you deserved to know at least what we know."

"Why would anyone bother going out there if she doesn't die?" Ben was having a hard time following the logic.

"She may not age, but she is mortal," Roger explained. "The stories left over from our fathers and theirs seem to agree that she can be killed. Only no one has yet succeeded."

Ben again took time to think things over. "Then I suppose my choice is made for me," he said. "I have to go out there."

"I would strongly advise against that," Roger said.

"You already have," Ben sighed, "but I can't leave without knowing the truth. Besides, if I can somehow stop this... thing... from doing what she's doing, then the world will be a better place. My friend is already in the city finding a boat; he should be here in a few hours, and we'll be leaving as soon as we can get it in the water."

Roger thought about arguing, but resigned himself to the will of a desperate man. "You should watch your step out there," he said simply. "Can I get you anything before you leave?"

"Yeah," said Ben. "You can tell me how to get there."

"Ah, of course," said Roger, clapping his hands once as if to jog his memory. "You will want to leave off of the western shore, and bear five or six degrees right of the sunset. The trip should take a few hours, but the island, once you are in sight of it, will be very hard to miss. Anything else?"

"No, thanks," said Ben, "there's someone I need to see before I go."

Roger nodded seriously. "Good luck, Ben."

He left Roger's house and walked up the stretch to find Micah. He wasn't sure which hut was his, but the search gave him time to put Roger's claims onto the mental rack, where everything was subject to scrutiny. He supposed that he wasn't entirely surprised by all the superstition given the kind of place Luna was, and it mattered little. All that mattered to him was that for whatever reason, Roger believed that his wife was on an island across the water, and he was going to investigate. Maybe he would get there and find a perfectly rational explanation for the myth, or maybe he would find a wretched little monster, all malevolence and ill will. Ben didn't care what he found as long as he found Lindsey.

After knocking on a few wrong doors and asking around, Ben was finally directed to Micah's hut. He was inside cleaning fish when Ben knocked on his door. Micah got up and opened it, his face reflecting nothing but that same sad, distant look that Ben remembered from the only other night he had spoken to him. "Good afternoon," he started, "you probably don't remember me, but I was hoping that I could have a word with you before I left tonight." Micah wiped his hands on his frayed burlap trousers and motioned Ben inside without hesitation. His voice, despite being so deep for an old timer's, was a bit sluggish and made his words sound ancient as he spoke.

"Please, of course, come in." He moved back to his cleaning table, not with the awkward shuffles that Ben was used to seeing in the elderly, but with a weathered stride that would have fit better in a palace hall, and sat down heavily in the poorly sanded wooden chair that matched the rest of the interior. "I remember you. How have you been getting along?"

"As well as I can, thank you," Ben answered. He didn't need to look around at the room to know that fish were everywhere but on the bed and the floor, either cleaned or soon-to-be. The hut absolutely reeked of them. "You sure have a lot of fish in here," he said, trying not to let on what a chore it was to choke back the pungent aroma.

"This is a fishing village," stated Micah, acknowledging the obvious. "And I am its most able artisan. I have done this for the people of Luna all my life." There was a long pause as he regarded Ben. "You can only be here for your wife," he guessed.

Ben appreciated the ice breaker's relevance. "Yes, Sir, that's right. I'm told that she may be nearby."

"So close, yet so far," said Micah enigmatically. "Were you also told about who is with her?"

"Actually, I was hoping to hear whatever you knew about it," Ben said. "I gather that your wife didn't drown."

Micah shook his head slowly. "No, no she did not." He picked up a fish and a knife and resumed his work. "Long ago, she was worshipped as a goddess here. She and her mate were a pair that the people of Luna could not explain; they were here before the first of us and it is believed that they were created and put here by a higher power. No way to be sure... they kept to themselves and never had any contact with the villagers unless by some mistake. At some point the Bitter One's mate acquired a taste for human women, and it was this that ultimately drove them apart. Heartbroken after finding him with women he had befriended, she flew into a rage and left in search of pure solitude, which she found. There she stayed, vowing never to let a truly happy union among humans go unpunished. At least, this is what my grandfather told me. As loving as the people are here, we are fortunate that she has not taken more than she has."

"What happened to her mate?" Ben wanted to know.

"No one really knows," said Micah. "They say he fled in fear of his wife's anger and never returned. And that is why she continues to torment us; her love never accepted responsibility for what he did, and she was never able to put it to rest. It would seem that even gods start out young," he said with a wry smile.

"Why didn't you go after her when she took your wife?" Ben asked.

Micah answered in a tired tone. "Wives were taken before mine, and wives have been taken after mine. I am the only one who did not pursue her, and I am the only one who is still here because of it." He pointed to the pile of fish in front of him, his friendly grin showcasing a full array of immaculately white teeth as he did so. "If I had gone, there would be no one here to clean all these fish."

Ben smiled, touched by the innocently noble remark. "Do you believe she's out there?" He asked finally.

Micah threw his current fish off to the side and picked up another one, never breaking stride in his work. "I believe that something is taking our people, and that is all I believe," he said. "But I think most of the others here would say differently. We have taken to naming her by her nature because we suspect those names seem to roll off our tongues easier than her real one would. Solitary, Bitter, Lonely—these are the things that will always be attached to her legacy among us. Sad that she has nothing else to live for, don't you think?"

Ben again thought about his own life over the last two years and nodded absently while Micah continued to clean his fish. "Why do you bother doing this in the first place if you eat with your hands right off of the bone?" He asked. "Is there something else you use all this fish meat for?" Micah looked up from his work, brow furrowed in puzzlement. "I remember Roger eating that way," he explained.

Micah grinned and went back to work. "Despite his fascination with expansion and the outside world, there are ways in which Roger is more primitive than the rest of us." He stopped cleaning and looked up, recalling. "Roger's origin is just as mysterious to us as the thing that waits for you across the water. I can remember when he arrived, a baby who had been abandoned by his parents. My father was fishing when he saw a basket floating not far off the shore and brought it in. Little did he know that his discovery would grow to play such a central part in our town."

"A strange origin," Ben said.

"Strange, indeed," said Micah. "It is a small miracle that he survived his journey at all. The gods work in mysterious ways. My father said that Roger was one of the brightest children he had ever met."

"I didn't ask him about it when I saw him earlier," Ben said. "But do you know whether or not he still plans on building this place up?"

"Oh, I'm sure he is," came the resigned reply. "Although I think that you were his last effort to find the money for it."

"How do the people in Luna feel about what he wants to do?" Ben asked. "How do *you* feel about it? Do you really want vacationers here all the time?"

"I can't say that I like the thought of my home becoming a tourist attraction," he answered. "But it may not turn out to be so bad. Besides," he said with the smile of someone who had long ago accepted fate, "I'm an old man, and the world is bound to move on eventually."

Ben spent the remainder of the afternoon in Micah's hut, and not just because the guy was such an engaging conversationalist. It seemed like the right time and place to prepare for whatever it was that lay ahead. He was about to dive head first into a void of uncertainty, and if you believed public opinion, he probably wasn't going to make it back. He found that he was a bit afraid, and he thought it was oddly humorous how strange things sometimes could be so comforting when he was scared. The cleaning of fish, for instance. He didn't know the slightest thing about it, nor had he ever watched anyone do it, but at the moment, sitting where he was and watching Micah clean those fish was the safest thing in the world to do. He wasn't in any rush to leave anymore; it was apparent to him that things would be unfolding on their own soon enough. Safety would be gone soon enough.

As late afternoon approached, Ben heard the distant sound of a diesel engine approaching the village and knew that transportation had arrived. He let out a deep breath and stood.

His host seemed to know that the time had come, and Ben watched thoughtfully while Micah reached into a nearby drawer and pulled out two leather bound hunting knives, each one eight inches in length, and offered them to Ben. "If you go there and find what you are looking for, you will need to protect yourself. Take these."

Ben took the weapons from Micah and fastened them to his belt at each side of his waist. Micah saw how well the ruggedness of the leather matched the ruggedness of Ben's clothing and nodded with approval. "Fitting," he said.

"Thank you for these," said Ben. "And for your time."

"Thank you for yours," replied Micah. "An old man cannot have enough visitors. You be careful out there." He turned back to his work and Ben headed out the door and back down the stretch. He found Chris waiting at the end of it with a pickup truck and a motorboat big enough to hold two people and not much else. The sun was setting by the time they pushed off, and Ben silently cursed himself for not waiting until daylight to make the trip. But there was nothing he could do; if Lindsey was out there, he couldn't let her suffer through one more minute of captivity than he had to. It had been long enough already.

Sun Setting

Chris dragged the boat up to shore as Ben collected himself and prepared to give chase.

"Will you be okay here?" Ben asked, turning his back to the wall and facing his friend.

"I'll be fine," Chris said. "I'll just be sitting here. *You* have to be careful." He pulled out the nine millimeter pistol they had packed and tossed it to Ben, who jammed it into his waistband.

"You know what to do if I'm not back by noon tomorrow?"

"Go back to Luna, find some authority, bring them here, storm the island, kill the monster."

"Right," said Ben. "Give it your best shot, anyway. You may not be taken seriously. Make sure you tell them what we saw just now." He started jogging down the beach and away from the boat.

"Where are you going?" Chris called. "Aren't you going to try and find a way up?"

"There *is* no way up here," Ben called back over his shoulder. "I don't have any time to waste. I'm going to see what's on the other side of this island and hope like hell something shows itself."

A few minutes of running down the beach and around the gentle bend that the wall made left Chris out of view and Ben already tired of running in sand.

His morale skyrocketed, however, as soon as he was able to see more of the island. He was thankful for the clear night and the full moon as he took in the view. From front to back, the island was one continuous, gradual slope, lowering itself until its surface elevation matched the beach. Reaching the island's top would require a detour, but fortunately no precarious climbing. He would simply have to start at the back and work his way up to the front.

Ben continued down the beach toward the back end of the island, guessing that the island itself was no more than a mile and a half long from tip to tip. If Lornamair intended to hide, it didn't look like she would have much room to maneuver. On the other hand, if she intended to kill him, he didn't have much room to maneuver, either. He didn't stop jogging until he was at the end of the island and looking in at an uninviting tangle of dense leaves and thorns that looked more like a solid wall than it did part of a forest. His calf muscles immediately retaliated against the unfamiliar running surface and he was forced to massage his legs for a minute before continuing, hoping that the setback wasn't a precursor to the kind of night he was going to have.

When he thought he was ready he looked around for the patch in the woods that seemed to harbor the fewest thorns and made his entry. The hospitality inside the forest more or less lived up to the promises it had made on the outside. Its huge leaves and jungle-like density didn't allow Ben to see much, and there were more than enough thorns in enough places to make it difficult to move without being shredded. The place wasn't impenetrable, but it wasn't far off it, either. Steps had to be taken gingerly to minimize the damage caused by the briars, and the ones closer to eye level had to be pinched just so. It wouldn't have taken so much effort if Ben had thought to pack long pants and gloves, but it would've been a full-fledged battle either way. Being so underdressed certainly didn't help, but he had taken his best guess about what to wear. The canopy almost made the full moon a non-factor, except for where there were inconsistent patches of clearing. Ben was no more than thirty feet in when he realized that he would never have been able to keep his bearing had it not been for the island's steady incline toward his destination. At no point was he allowed to take a regular step, and it was soon apparent that it was going to be a fight the entire way. As bothersome as all this was, though, the most unsettling part about everything was that the forest was dead silent. If there were any birds there they weren't making any noise, there were no insects chirping, no tiny forest creatures scurrying. The only sounds Ben heard were made by his own rustling of the forest and the distant waves breaking violently on the shore and against the natural walls of the island.

As creepy as it was, it was just as well as far as Ben was concerned. Once he thought about it, the absence of wildlife wasn't all that surprising. How was anything supposed to get there? Besides, silence was better to think in than the racket that was supposedly customary for a jungle-like environment. It made him feel safer, knowing that it would be virtually impossible for something (or someone) to creep up on him. There were times, fairly frequent ones, at which he had to stop and rest his burning muscles. His legs felt the worst; between the steady incline and the unforgiving tangle of vines that smothered the forest floor, he was getting quite a workout. Though he took these breaks reluctantly, they gave him chances to try to put together the things that didn't quite make sense.

His thoughts consistently returned to Roger. Ben had been more than slightly miffed to learn that Roger had had theories about his wife's fate as early as the night she disappeared, but he could understand someone's unwillingness to offer such lunacy into the discussion immediately. There was a good chance that it only would have made Ben angry anyway, that he would have written it off as irrelevant superstition and turned his attention to people who had more viable things to say. But *two years?* Two years seemed like a lot of time to let elapse before finally acting on an attack of conscience. If Roger had felt bad about not saying anything immediately, it felt wrong that it would have taken that long to succumb to his conscience. If he *hadn't* had immediate regrets, it felt wrong that it would have taken so long to find some. Either there would be regrets, or there wouldn't. And no man with a conscience would be foolish or patient enough to wait *two years* before speaking up. In short, something just felt wrong.

Ben shook his head clear and started moving again, the burning in his calves having subsided for now. There would be time to sort it all out, but that time would come after he had found his wife.

All things considered, the first leg of his trek was blissfully uneventful despite the difficult terrain. His legs were aching badly from walking uphill all night and stung because of all the cuts that the thorns had already administered. His arms and face weren't in much better condition, and the tiny clearing he stumbled into after fighting off the latest assault on his clothing by a thorn-covered tree came as a welcome surprise. He sat down roughly and wiped the sweat from his face with the sleeve of his tee shirt, grateful that the darkness didn't let him see how much blood came with it. He took out the thorns that he found in his arms, legs, and clothes and leaned back on his hands, looking at the clearing because there was nothing else to see. It was just a sliver of relief in a maze of pain, an untainted haven of mercy that Ben thought the Devil must have overlooked when he drew up his plans for the island. He sat on one end of the oblong shaped ring, which wasn't big enough to allow him to feel comfortable. It was long, but slender; as soon as he was ready to take a few more steps up the hill he would be plunged back into the thick of the forest. There were leaves from the ground to the canopy in broken patterns, not allowing Ben to see anything outside of the clearing. There were saplings surrounding it, which he thought was strange considering how long the forest had surely been there. His eyes brushed over the leaves at the end of the clearing and his heart stopped when he noticed the gentle, waving pattern of what looked like human hair.

It wasn't exactly light, and it wasn't exactly dark. Moonlight slid down the length of it like a spider's silk, accentuating its curves and lending it a pale shade that whispered of a supernatural quality. It was all the colors of a tree in mid-autumn—a few locks of weathered blonde faded softly into darker shades of auburn, scorched orange, and black, only to gradually emerge again like the creeping chill of a late October morning. It was ghostly, and beautiful—and strange, and threatening. Ben sat in silence and traced the contours of the mysterious mane with his eyes, starting at the tips and winding his way up along the peculiar edges of black streaks set against the lighter hues of fall, up and around where one might expect a scalp to be, and down a few inches to… a hairline.

He squinted hard and tried to focus through the visual static that came at night for those who didn't make a habit of sitting in darkness. His eyes were about as adjusted as they were going to get, and the moonlight, while bright in the sky, offered little help in the shadows it cast at the edge of the clearing. But after a moment, yes, there it was—the outline of a face, the gentle curves of a woman's cheekbones, and a slender, delicate jawline, all framed by the silky cascade of seasonal color that had first caught his attention. Another moment drifted past, and the contours of a youthful face were pieced together by the dim light and his mind's reflexive image closure. Before he had a chance to wonder why there was a head suspended in the jungle, the body materialized beneath it.

The thick leaves and the blackish-blue hue that settled over everything—not to mention the lack of daylight—made it hard to determine what exactly it was that he was seeing, but the truth made itself clear soon enough. A woman's arms were raised gracefully over her head, fluidly weaving in and out, like the rest of her body, with the leaves and vines that ended the clearing. Even after she knew that Ben's eyes had locked in on her she stayed motionless, half immersed in the jungle and standing with the confidence and territorial stubbornness of someone who could only be the owner of the island. On her face was a look of calm superiority, a condescending mask of unidentifiable feelings made eerie by the moonlight. She was a cat who knew that her mouse had never had a chance, and her theatrical pose struck Ben as more than just camouflage. Every detail of the encounter had been orchestrated, from the place, manner, and situation right down to the blood and sweat on his face and arms; it was an elephant in the room, the unspoken secret the two strangers shared as their gazes pressed against the other's will, waging a psychological battle that Ben instinctively knew he couldn't win.

For Ben, coming to the island had been a matter of life or death; the journey had given him the hope that he would be able to put his life back together, and with that hope came the risk of dying young. But he was here, wasn't he? He was here, unmindful of the risk and ready to move the Earth in order to take back the most important thing in his universe—that precious commodity which life had so mercilessly stolen from him those two years earlier—love. And the earth *would* move, wouldn't it…? *Wouldn't it?* In his hasty and single-minded pursuit of his wife, he hadn't doubted it for a second; how could the Earth *not* move, when he felt so strongly? But now he was in the thick of it, and in Lornamair's flawless, moonlit complexion, he caught his first glimpse of reality. She didn't care why he was there any more than people cared about the business of insects, and she certainly had no intention of being moved simply by Ben's dedication and force of will, no matter how strong. She had no reason to even take him seriously, and that realization made Ben's heart race for a hundred reasons at once, but most of all because of the helplessness he felt when he thought about how long she had probably been watching him.

Lornamair lowered her arms slowly and steadily, making no sound among the leaves she had entwined as she ceremoniously untangled herself from them in a subtle but well-versed dance, her eyes never leaving

Ben's as she did so. Her legs followed suit shortly after and she took a single, deliberate step forward, pulling herself out of the forest and into the full moonlight with all the elegance of a ballroom dancer and the calculated speed of a cobra who hadn't yet decided to strike. When her feet were together, she slid one of them forward slightly and brought it to rest with the ball of the foot on the ground and her heel in the air, as if she was wearing one high-heeled shoe that he couldn't see. She then turned her upper body a bit and put one hand on her forward hip, pushing one delicate shoulder in Ben's direction and holding it there while she continued to look down on him. He almost expected her to roll that shoulder like a barroom singer would (the pose was almost perfect), but his wariness and the potential bleakness of the situation didn't let him indulge in such frivolous thoughts for long. The entrancing process left Ben spellbound until the cat finally spoke to her mouse.

"I felt your blood freeze," she whispered. She leaned back against a tree and embraced it as though it was a lover enfolding her from behind. Her eyes closed and she turned her face toward the sky, drawing in a deep breath and letting it out with a soft, sultry groan. "It was wonderful."

"Jesus," Ben said, transfixed and a little awestruck. "You're beautiful."

Lornamair arched her back and parted her lips ever so slightly, easing away from the tree and out of the shadows. When she opened her eyes and looked down at Ben, a new feature both startled and mesmerized him—irises as clear, green, and piercing as polished emeralds. "And you're a fool," she seethed, "for intruding in places to which you were not invited." Her voice was silky, and totally devoid of the tropical accent he was accustomed to hearing on the mainland. It was such perfect English it was startling, really.

"I don't mean any disrespect," Ben replied. "If you're the one who owns this island, then I'm completely at your mercy. I've come for my wife."

Lornamair narrowed her eyes as she purred her response. "No one owns an island, fool. Ownership is a bedtime story humans tell each other in order to mitigate their insignificance. And you should be careful what you wish for," she advised.

"Let her go," Ben said, ignoring the strange remark. "I'm just asking that you let her go, and you'll never hear from either of us again."

Lornamair's body melted back into its empress-like stance. "No," she said quietly.

"I don't want conflict," Ben said. "I really don't. But I can't leave without my wife. I simply don't have a choice. Please, let her go."

Lornamair cocked her head to one side, her gaze perfectly expressionless at first. Then her eyes softened, then narrowed, then lost their expression again. Then her brow furrowed, then it relaxed, then there was just a flash of a smile, then a snarl, then nothing again. She cocked her head to the other side. When she spoke again, her words were plain and genuinely quizzical. "You don't have a pulse," she said, much to Ben's confusion. She put a hand on her waist and looked herself over, then she looked down at Ben and gave him a full body scan, then back at herself, then finally back to Ben. "Is it my clothes?"

Ben, keeping both eyes on the strange but alluring newcomer, put one hand over his heart to make sure it was still beating, which, of course, it was. "I don't understand," he said. "Did you make those yourself?"

Until she had mentioned it, Ben hadn't noticed how odd her clothing really was. "You have a lot of talent."

Her garb appeared to be almost entirely made of burlap—the same material many pieces of clothing were spun from on the mainland. To say that she was wearing rags would have been fair; her shirt was nothing more than a wide swatch of material with a hole cut in the center for her head, with a cut made down the front, presumably to keep the fabric from irritating her neck. It simply rested on her shoulders, and the sides were open but stitched together by some kind of twine, which hugged the makeshift shirt/vest/tunic tight to her body. It was tucked into a skirt about knee length, which had clearly been cut from the same pattern as the top. A wide swatch, this one cut completely in half, hung from another piece of twine wrapped around her waist that served as a functional belt and waistband, leaving her thighs naked at the sides. It was all in a very earthy tone, and therefore excellent camouflage.

Lornamair furrowed her brow and narrowed her eyes once more, as though trying to solve a complicated math problem. As quickly as the expression came, it was gone. "No pulse, but terribly anxious," she purred. She took a step forward and leaned in a bit; she was fairer-skinned than the people on the mainland, and the moonlight made her look otherworldly. "I wonder, what else is in there?"

Ben whipped the pistol out of his waistband and pointed it with an unsteady hand at what he thought was about to be an attacker. "Don't come any closer," he ordered.

Lornamair never looked at the gun. She inhaled sharply and threw her head back, bringing her hands up and running them through her hair as she let out an erotic-sounding "Ooooohhhhhh" that ended in a passionate exhale. When she looked down again at Ben, her eyes were excited. She pushed her tongue a short way through her slightly-parted lips, then withdrew it. *"There's* something," she breathed.

Ben's heart was racing, and his hand was shaking, and her obvious disregard for his threats only made it worse. Her eyes stayed steady on his as her words continued to drip from her mouth like syrup, saturating his mind like a heavy rainforest mist. "You shouldn't threaten me," she said. "I can see your soul from here." Her eyes relaxed, and her mouth curled into an unfriendly smile. "Ohhhhh, it must be so hard," she said with what had to be mock sympathy, "not wanting to trust me, but knowing that I'm the only hope you have of finding what you came for."

"This island isn't that big," Ben said. "And I'll turn it upside down if I have to, with or without you."

"That's an awful lot of conviction for a man with no pulse," Lornamair said, the expression of fake sincerity on her face ascending into melodrama. "But you don't know anything about where you are. How deep does it go? Tell me exactly, Ben—where has your love gone?"

Another chill went up Ben's spine, and Lornamair closed her eyes a moment, pleasure touching the corners of her mouth. When she opened them again, he finally spoke. "How is it that you know my name?"

"Obviously, I've been spending time with someone who knows you," she answered. "She's fine, by the way. She told me you would come eventually...if we can agree to play nice, I can take you to her."

Ben's heart skipped a beat, and Lornamair's eyelids fluttered, ever so slightly. "Why do I feel like you're jerking me around?" He wanted to know. "What are you getting out of this?"

"Is that how you treat everyone who makes you such a generous offer?" She said, looking wounded. Her face then softened, and she raised her hands as if to show that she was unarmed. "If I wanted to hurt you, don't you think I would have a weapon?" She turned a slow three-hundred-and-sixty degrees and once again came to a stop facing Ben. Slowly, gracefully, she lowered herself down to her hands and knees, and started crawling toward him in a roundabout, circular pattern as wide as the small clearing would allow. He grabbed the gun with his other hand to steady his aim as he watched her patiently and deliberately work her way over to where he sat with all the sleekness and elegance of an exotic jungle cat. "Tst tst tst tst," she said, as she pulled her face within inches of his. "We both know you don't want to use this. You don't need it. I am not your enemy." She put one delicate hand on top of Ben's handgun and slowly lowered it until it pointed at the dirt. Ben sat through all of it, nervous, mesmerized, and completely lost in that sea of crystal green, glossy obsidian, and untainted white that were Lornamair's reassuring eyes. "May I?" She asked, gently pulling the nine millimeter out of his grip. It didn't feel right, and it didn't feel wrong, so he didn't fight it. With a flourished flick of her wrist, she tossed the gun into the woods—only a few yards, but far enough to be lost forever in that mess. "Isn't that better?" She asked rhetorically. "Now maybe we can handle this like adults. I'm going to turn around and crawl back to where I was. Can I trust you not to hurt me?"

Ben gave no response, and Lornamair didn't wait for one. She turned, every bit as slowly as she had come, and went back to her end of the clearing following the same circular path she had taken before. Ben watched the muscles in her thighs tense, relax, and ripple with each crawling step she took, a reflex which, for the first time since her arrival, he had to remind himself to ignore.

She reached the other end of the clearing and stood, letting out a long, audible sigh. "Almost," she said. Then, looking over her shoulder, told Ben, "Follow me if you really want to see your wife. I can see the forest has already worn you down; those cuts must be stinging by now. I can get you through safely, but you have to get up first."

Ben pushed himself unsteadily to his feet and took a couple of steps toward her. "Thank you for your—"

Before he could properly express his gratitude, his stomach jumped up into his throat. In the same moment he realized that the ground had just disappeared from under him, something rough and sharp ripped through his shorts and took an unhealthy amount of meat out of his thigh. Ben landed brutally on his back, expecting to be dead and very grateful that he wasn't. Other sticks hadn't missed the rest of his body by much, but they had missed. His breathing was stuttered and sharp as he writhed as much as he could, his wide open eyes not seeing anything but the red and black flashes of pain that accompanied the wound in his leg.

Lornamair leaned over the edge and sighed when she saw that Ben hadn't been completely skewered. "I suppose the pit will be needing more sticks in the future, then," she said to Ben, whose mind was in other places. She turned and left without saying anything else, leaving Ben there to die.

It was a few minutes before Ben could think clearly enough to act. The moonlight was his only aid as he used nearby spikes to pull himself to a sitting position. He spread the tear in his shorts enough to assess the damage to his leg, and after tearing off one of his shirt sleeves and wiping as much of the blood away as he could he decided that it could have been worse. There was no question it would need stitches, but obviously that would have to wait. He backed himself up against the wall of the pit and held the wound closed with his hands, applying pressure and fuming at what had just happened. She had no reason to take him seriously. She had home field advantage, and every time Ben tried to seem threatening it was likely to get thrown back in his face, as it just had. She had known he didn't want to pull the trigger, and she had known just what to do to ensure that he didn't. No one liked being an open book, especially when the stakes were this high.

Moon Rising

"Nnnnnggggggghhhhh!" The pull was excruciating, but there was freedom above, death below, and no quarter to be taken in between. Ben hung suspended from Micah's two hunting knives, thrust into the dense dirt wall of the pit that had almost claimed his life shortly before. With a vice grip on the knife in his left hand, he yanked it out of the wall and plunged it back in over his head, feeling the sweat in his palm cause his right hand to slip a little down the smooth finish of the knife it was gripping. *"Ergh!"* A few more quick breaths, and… *"Nnnnnnggggggghhhhhhaaaahhh!"* The back of his mind was aware of the dirt getting smeared into the still-open wound in his leg, but it was one of many unpleasantries that would have to wait until he had reached the top before being addressed. Out came the lower knife, the one on the right this time, and back in it went, over his head. His right shoulder screamed; maybe the fall had injured that, too. Christ, that thing was deep. He looked up for a second. *Two more,* he thought, *three if my luck doesn't change.* Out came the left knife, and back in overhead. *"Nnnnnnnggggggghhhhhhhaaa!"* His eyes blazed with pain, but saw nothing as he once again pulled himself higher. His breath had nearly left him,

taken by the fear of what failing to reach the top of that pit would mean; there was little to no chance he would survive that fall twice, and the damned finish on those knives was hell bent on using his own sweat to stamp out his chances of survival. But sure enough, he was close enough to the top now to reach over and plant the next knife in the ground over the edge. His mind was beyond coherent thought, his muscles were near failure, and he knew his shoulder wouldn't like it, but he took out the lower knife and swung it in a wide arc, planting it in the ground over the pit's edge. He tried to suppress a scream as tears streamed out of his eyes uncontrollably, but the knife was in. Shaking his head and blinking back the water, he began what would be his last upward pull—only to have the knife over the edge cut through the loose dirt like it was butter. Dirt shot into his wide open eyes and the knife exploded out of the top of the wall, suddenly leaving him with only the grip in his left hand between him and death. He flailed his right arm backwards and the momentum almost carried him off the wall. He planted the knife back into the wall and hung there, trying to find an elevation at which he could hang and give his arms something that resembled rest. He sobbed once, and the only word he could manage out loud came out in a squeezed plea for mercy. *"Aahhh."* He didn't trust his right shoulder to hold while he tried for a better plant with the left. It would have to be the right. Now blind and beyond desperate, Ben ripped the right knife out of the wall and, with a Herculean effort, lifted himself with his left arm the couple of inches he needed to reach completely over the top and plant the knife a solid foot beyond the first attempt. He tugged on it once, but knew he didn't have time to be picky; he was going up now or never. He pulled, and swung his right leg up and over the edge. He then squirmed the rest of his body over the top, leaving only his left arm and leg dangling against the wall. Face down and inhaling dirt off the forest floor, he was incapable of celebration. There was only pain, and it would be more than a few minutes before it subsided enough to move. It occurred to him, distantly, that if Lornamair were to show up for some reason and kick him back down there, there was nothing he was going to do about it. His luck needed to hold if he was going to survive.

A few minutes later, a deep breath let Ben know that he had caught his second wind. He rolled over onto his back and away from the edge, taking the other knife out with him. Laying there, he put both knives in their sheaths and snapped them shut. His shoulder was searing, his leg was throbbing, but his hands went to his head, which was crushing the sanity out of him. So much strain had probably broken a blood vessel. Still, painful or not, he had to move. If Lornamair was going to come back to finish the job, she would at least have to suffer the inconvenience of dragging him some distance through those blasted briars. He rolled over onto his stomach, blind and nearly delirious, and laughed the mad, devil-may-care laugh of someone who had just cheated Death himself. He wiped his eyes on his shoulders, ignoring the pain, and blinked a few times. His eyes stayed open, and that was good enough.

He crawled in the direction in which Lornamair had tossed his gun; you never knew, maybe he'd find it. When he got to the edge of the clearing, he proceeded like someone trying to infiltrate a prison camp (which wasn't all that far from the truth). He stayed low to the ground, pecked and prodded for larger openings in the briars, and made the best out of what he had. After several feet in, he gave up searching for the gun. He'd never find it. It was just too damned hard to see anything, nevermind move. He reached out and scraped some leaves together in a pile, which he then rested his head on. Closing his eyes, he could only hope the island's queen didn't have a reason to go back to the pit before he woke. *Old witch, huh?* He thought to himself. All the ghost stories had prepared him for ugly and mean— what he found instead was beautiful and deadly. *And for a minute there, she seemed so nice,* he thought, chuckling to himself.

He awoke sometime after, but as sleep always was for him now, it felt no longer than a moment. The pain was duller, but he didn't feel rested. The moon hadn't made it halfway across the sky and already the island had knocked him down and counted to ten. It wasn't something he wanted to admit, but his random thoughts gave his weariness away. He would never have thought so yesterday, but now? Lord knew, if he had had any idea what was waiting for him out here there was actually a small chance he never would have climbed into that boat—Ben's blood suddenly felt a freezing pulse of panic and he cut his breath short, because for some reason he felt it helped him think more clearly. Frantically he rummaged through his memory, as though it was an old closet that hid something forgotten and valuable at the bottom.

Ben's brain, reflex organ that it was, had tripped over a chain of thoughts springing from the word "boat," and ending at what he thought could have been another piece of the puzzle. He sent his mind back two years to the night of the disappearance. He remembered asking Roger about how a kidnapper could get to Luna. He remembered suggesting by water, or more to the point, by boat. Then he remembered Roger's response: *The rocks out there do not allow it,* he had said. Ben, at the time, didn't have a reason to question Roger's integrity, and didn't think to investigate for himself. He thought about the brief conversations he had had with the officer in charge—Mathis, his name was—and couldn't recall an instance of anyone present directly referencing an approach to Luna by boat. At that point, he had already suggested it to Roger, and, not having a reason to doubt, never brought it up again. It was possible that Mathis regarded the possibility of a water approach as a given, and therefore wouldn't have a reason to bring it up, either. Ben couldn't remember the conversation well enough to be sure, but there was one thing about which he was positive—he and Chris had *left* Luna by boat to come to this infernal island, no more than eight hours ago. Where were all the rocks that prevented boating? Removed within the last two years? His thoughts kept racing, each of them in a dead heat to be the first one that arrived at the truth. The closer he felt he was getting, the faster they came. He had been told by— had it been Roger or Micah?—that there had been people who had come here to retrieve their wives in the past; what did they do, swim? No chance; the trip by boat had been entirely too far. Ben no longer suspected that he hadn't been told everything. Now he *knew* that he hadn't been told everything. He also thought he knew who hadn't told him. What he couldn't put together, of course, was why. If Roger had known two years ago what had happened, and that he could possibly do something about it, why withhold information? *Because he didn't want me here then,* said his voice of reason. And now? *Now he does.*

Ben grimaced as he slowly pushed himself into a sitting position and looked around. Roger wanted him there, and Lornamair knew he was there. There was still a lot that he didn't understand about his situation, but for a moment it didn't matter. For a moment, he was convinced that he was there to die. There was no way to sneak around, and his new enemy already knew where he was. In that moment, everything was hopeless. When the moment had passed, he remembered that no matter what anyone else's reasons for sending him there were, he had reasons of his own. The time for figuring it all out, again, would come later. *Now move.*

Ben forced himself back up and further into the Hellish forest with sheer determination and rage lending strength to his tired limbs. His legs immediately ached again when he began ungracefully plodding along through the foliage, which would have seemed more in its place in a nightmare.

All over again he was swallowed by a maze of thorns in a sea of leaves. Ben's labored steps became the only clock he knew, a clock that was unreliable at best. He decided that time hardly mattered now, anyway. Besides, it wasn't yet dawn, which meant that he still had at least several hours before Chris would leave without him. Even though his injured leg made every next step seem impossible to take, he continued to take them, plowing through entangling vines and brushing off briars that snared his clothing and skin with each one. The island was intent on stopping Ben's advance but he kept pressing on, injured, mostly blind, tired, and furious. He knew that each step up the incline was one more step closer to his goal, and each one felt like a success. After about seven hundred successes that found him lost at some unknown point in the forest, his progress was halted by the sound of a twig snapping off to his right.

Ben instantly froze and took one of the knives out of its sheath, holding it at his side and preparing to lacerate whatever moved in his direction. He had known that it was just a matter of time before Lornamair figured out that he was still alive. He had also known that he wasn't difficult to track, so he wasn't surprised when she had apparently caught up with him—he had expected it, even. What made him nervous was the fact that he had been able to hear anything at all. He had seen how the island witch was able to move; if she didn't want to make a sound, she wouldn't have. Which meant that she *wanted* him to hear her approach. The sound had been a stone's throw away, but the island's deathly silence made it seem much closer. He hunkered down slowly and silently, his face pained as his wounded leg resisted the pressure. As he stared in the direction of the noise it repeated itself, a bit closer than before, and more toward his left. His eyes darted in that direction as he strained to hear something, anything, that might reveal her location positively. Another light snapping sound at his two o'clock, or maybe it was a small object striking the ground, and his eyes darted again as he tried to will a line of sight through the huge leaves blocking his vision and a light source stronger than the moon into the forest, but all in vain. Ben fought back another wave of panic, a feeling that was becoming more and more second nature to him on Lornamair's island. *For all I know, she's behind me throwing stones,* he thought anxiously. Soon, though, the sounds seemed to centralize directly in front of him, still relatively far away, and quickened playfully. Ben was reminded of a child tapping out a rhythm that only he could hear, and simultaneously became more nervous and angry, feeling again like a mouse in a trap that he couldn't see. Momentarily the individual sounds turned into footfalls, a startlingly heavy sound pounded out in a slow and ominous beat. It was the sound of someone walking on fallen leaves and packed dirt, which struck Ben as odd since he hadn't yet found an opportunity to take a comfortable step. As terrified as he was, he knew that all he had to do was time his strike with whatever was approaching, which was doubtlessly Lornamair. Once the footsteps had closed half the distance, they quickened, and Ben's heartbeat rose with them. Then, with no other warning, the steps broke into a run as though there was no forest to fight at all and Ben gripped the hilt of his knife, ready to lunge. At the moment he thought that she would come crashing through the brush in front of him, he stood and stabbed in the same motion—but the knife only found air. The footfalls had come to a sudden stop and Ben froze, knowing that she was just on the other side of the veil of leaves that had all along inhibited his vision, no more than four feet in front of him. There was a moment of silence—and then something kicked the back of his knees outward, making him fall flat on his back and lose the air in his lungs. Almost before he had even landed, and long before he had the opportunity to wonder how in the hell she moved so quickly, he felt the knife at the other side of his waist leave its sheath. He opened his dazed eyes just in time to register an upside-down image of the weapon raised over Lornamair's head. With all the strength he could muster he kicked in a backwards somersault-like motion and caught her squarely in the face before she could drive the blade down and into his chest. Lornamair let out a grunt and dropped the knife, momentarily stunned and falling backwards from the impact. Still keeping a firm grip on his own knife, Ben wasted no time in rolling over onto his stomach and stabbing at the foot of his assailant, which was the most readily available thing to strike. Lornamair pulled her foot away with startling speed and was gone, leaving Ben alone with another knife planted in the ground and a racing heart. This time he didn't stall; he hobbled to his feet and started moving in the same direction he thought she had gone in, as quickly as the forest was willing to allow. There was no time to calm his nerves and check his fresh wounds; he wasn't going to survive by trying to hide from her. He had to try to throw her out of her comfort zone by taking the fight to her before she had a chance to orchestrate another trick or get the drop on him. She could be hurt, at least he was now able to confirm that much. And if she could be hurt, he had more of a chance than he had first thought.

Moon Falling

Moving quickly took its toll. Ben wasn't taking the time to pry the thorns out of his clothes or skin, instead letting them tear whatever they got a hold of. He had been following Lornamair's footfalls for an impossible length of time. He was convinced he was approaching his physical limit; thoughts came in spurts, and he was insanely tired of every cursed step bringing flashes of pain to his entire being for some reason or another. And now, he didn't even get to dictate his own pace. He had to stay close. He tripped over roots and banged his knees against trees, not caring about the bruises they would leave and letting his frustration push him through all the island's obstacles until several minutes later, when that all-too-familiar burn in his muscles returned and he collapsed face down in a heap. The first thing he noticed when his breathing slowed after a moment was how loud the crashing of waves seemed after so much silence. He rolled over onto his back and opened his eyes, seeing that his vision wasn't being hindered by the canopy. What he saw was an awe-inspiring starlit sky, showcasing the light source which was, besides Chris, the only thing that he could consider a friend while on the island—the full moon. Seeing it fully for the first time was seeing hope incarnate, but he had to notice that it was about three quarters of the way through its nightly jaunt across the sky. In a couple of hours it would be dawn, which would mean that time was shorter, but at least he would be able to see his way around.

Again the crashing waves demanded his attention. Was the forest really that dense, that that kind of noise couldn't penetrate? He supposed it must have been. He raised his head stiffly and saw that he had found the edge of one side of the island, the right side as you looked at it from the back. He no longer heard Lornamair's footsteps. By another unlikely stroke of luck, he was still alive; if he hadn't collapsed, there was a decent chance he would have run right off the side of the island. *She tried to walk me off a cliff. Oh, that bitch.* He noted that the ground he had collapsed onto was not covered with leaves or vines, but was instead bare, packed dirt. The foliage didn't cover this part of the island, it seemed, at least not this close to the edge. The island's signature breeze lightly swept at his hair, turning the sheen of sweat on his forehead to salt that felt scratchy when he wiped at it. He crawled to the edge wearily and looked over. It was quite a drop, and the sight of it told him that he couldn't be very far from his destination. The area was clear enough to let him look up the side of the island, and he saw the hill that he and Chris had seen from the other side when he had arrived.

Just a little farther, he thought, *to the top.*

His thoughts (more likely it was just *one* thought, for at that point his mind was only capable of one thought at a time) were interrupted by the nearby sound of something metal dragging against stone; reflexively he got to one knee, startled and looking for something to stab. His eyes locked with those of a girl sitting on a large rock behind what looked like a stone well protruding a few feet out of the ground. The moisture on her face glistened in the moonlight and ran in tracks down her dark, young-looking skin. She was wearing a gown the color of sea foam which almost glowed as the moon hit it. When Ben looked more closely he saw that she was chained to the side of the well by a single manacle attached to one of her ankles, and immediately he knew that he was looking at one of Lornamair's prisoners.

"I don't suppose you could get off that rock and give me a hand," Ben said. The exhaustion in his voice seemed to relax the girl a bit; a tired voice was not a threatening one.

She shook her head, her eyes reflecting her uncertainty. "She keeps the keys with her." Her voice was light and unassuming, and even having the kind of night he was having, Ben could appreciate beauty when he saw it. Long, straight, black hair complemented dark but luminous eyes set in a face that, under different circumstances, would have looked more at home in a calendar.

Ben, who hadn't expected anything to begin with, simply nodded downward and, after putting his knife away, said, "How long have you been here?"

The girl considered the question, but only shook her head again. "I don't know. Years, certainly."

With a huge effort Ben stood and tiredly shuffled his way to the well, where he plopped down near the girl and propped himself up against the side. He continued his interrogation in a low, nearly exhausted voice. "You're from Luna?"

The girl's uncertain stare held firm, as if to say *What kind of a question is that?* "I'm just wondering," Ben explained, "if there's anything else I don't know about this mess. I was told that before my wife, she hadn't abducted any outsiders."

"You're here for your wife?" The girl asked.

This time it was Ben's turn to look bewildered. "Is there another reason for someone to be out here?" The girl stayed silent, staring. "Why does she do it?" He asked.

"Did you come out here knowing nothing?" The girl wanted to know, her voice incredulous. "You didn't find your way here on your own; no one could have. Were you told nothing?"

"Seems more and more that way every time I take a step," Ben said with a sigh. "Why did she take you?" He asked again, hoping to find out about Lornamair's exploits from someone who had direct experience.

"Because she's jealous," the girl said bitterly, the hint of tears forming in her eyes. "Because she doesn't want anyone to be happy." It was the only consistent piece of the puzzle he had, the only answer that everyone seemed to share.

"It's a shame that's her only reason," said Ben. "All this trouble she goes to hardly seems worth it." He stood up gingerly and started looking himself over. "Has she ever said anything about letting you go?"

Ben could hear the girl's angry smile as she spoke. "Oh yes, I can go as soon as my tears fill up this well." Ben stopped and looked at her, then took a few steps toward the well and looked down. It wasn't deep as far as wells went, definitely not deep enough for extracting water, so it was hardly a news flash when he didn't see a drop of water in it. What he saw instead was the startling image of a dirty human skeleton at the bottom, its legs over its head in a position that Ben was sure had been instantly fatal. He was more interested in the Sisyphus-like task, however, than he was in the bones.

"Why is she making you fill up the well?"

"She won't accept my apology without proof of sincerity," the girl said.

"You mean she won't believe you're sorry until you feel badly enough about what you did that you cry enough to fill the well?"

The girl nodded, and then added solemnly, "I'm going to die here."

Ben paused before pressing further. "May I ask what it is that you did to wind up here? What is it that she wants an apology for?"

The girl looked away from Ben for the first time since he had arrived, clearly reluctant to answer his question. After a few moments, the answer finally came. "Getting married."

Ben had heard about enough, and he felt his face flush with anger again as he asked his next question. "And who is that down there?" He asked, referring to the set of bones in the well. He was hoping for a dozen answers other than the one he expected, but didn't get any of them.

"My husband," she said, beginning to cry openly. "He came here to take me home." She closed her eyes and started to rock back and forth gently, all the while fidgeting with her hands as years of despair and buried emotions caught up with her at once. *"How could she…"* the girl started to ask, but ultimately was unable to find the right words to describe what exactly Lornamair had done to her life. *"I don't want to be here…"* she trailed off into a whispery whine that left Ben resolute, pained for her and determined to bring her some peace.

He sat down on the rock next to her and put an arm around her, staring at the ground and finding himself at a total loss for what to say. "You aren't going to die here," he said finally. The girl sniffed and wiped her eyes, trying to collect herself. "I promise that if I live through this, I'll get you home."

"Thank you," she said quietly. "But you're just as dead as I am."

"That may be," Ben answered. "But that isn't something that I'm going to sit here and accept as fact."

"You're very brave," said the girl. "Your wife is lucky to have you. How long has it been since she was taken?"

"It's been two years," Ben said darkly.

"Probably still in the Den," said the girl. "Probably most recent. She'll be there until the old witch takes another, as I was before she came."

"So you know where I can find her?" He asked.

"You can find the Den in the side of the hill near the front of the island," she answered. "It isn't far from here. It's where she keeps us when we first arrive. I was the last one there before the new one moved me out."

Lindsey... Ben thought.

It sounded as though Lindsey's story would be comparable to—

"What's your name?" Ben asked the girl.

"Mehya," she said, now with dry eyes.

"If I'm alive when the sun comes up," he said again, standing and putting a hand on her shoulder, "I promise I'll get you out of here."

The girl looked up at him affectionately, making no attempt to contain her concern for his wellbeing. "Good luck, then," she said.

Ben took a few steps away and the entire scene went to Hell. He was about to reenter the forest when a pair of hands shot out of the thick foliage at ground level and yanked his feet out from under him. Again Lornamair had him on the ground with a sickening thud, and Mehya cried out in dismay at seeing her chance of getting off the island stamped out. Lornamair didn't give Ben time to recover as she stood over him and grabbed him by his hair, dragged him to the edge of the well, and pushed him in head first before he had ever had a chance to realize what was happening. He hit the bottom face first, hearing multiple things in his neck and back fracture, but realizing that the fall hadn't killed him. Mehya again cried in protest when she heard the skeleton of her dead husband shatter under Ben's weight, but her screams were cut short by a ferociously audible slap in the face from her captor. Even with the gritty taste of age-old dirt in his mouth, Ben had the presence of mind to know that he was looking at the best chance he would ever have to get Lornamair off his trail. He drew an unimaginably painful breath in and held it, willing himself not to move despite his agony. Lornamair came to the edge of the well and looked in to find Ben's body unmoving and upside down in an awkward slump against its wall. Ben continued to hold his breath, all too aware of the dull sound of blood pumping in his head and the veins throbbing in his face, praying that she would soon lose interest and decide that she had finally made a successful attempt on his life. Lornamair, having learned from their first two encounters that Ben was a bit more resilient than she was used to, found a rock the size of her head and threw it down the well at him. It struck him on the side, fortunately not a direct blow, and though the scraping of skin and the cracking of ribs made it harder than ever for him not to move, he stayed still. His deliberate silence magnified the gut-wrenching sound of more of his bones being smashed, and the final thud made by the rock landing inches from his head made him doubt for an instant whether or not he had indeed survived. Having seen enough, Lornamair turned and went out of her way to strike her prisoner's face with her open hand again before going back into the forest, not lowering herself to speak to someone who was in chains.

Ben started breathing again when he heard the second slap, knowing that Lornamair's attention was elsewhere. She hadn't bothered with stealth when she went back into the forest, thinking that Ben had finally been killed, and he listened as her rustling of leaves became distant. When he thought it was safe to move, he started by rolling onto the back of his neck into a more natural position. Every bone in his body screamed, but some of the pain subsided after he had settled. He used his elbows to work his way up into a sitting position, slowly letting his legs slide down the wall and snaking his back up the other side. Cursing everything on the island for being so enclosed, he stopped fighting once he had gotten himself to sit cross legged at the bottom of the well. Everything on that island was a fight. He found that it was too painful to turn his head to the left and that it hurt to straighten his back, so he was extra careful about standing. The well looked easy to climb out of; the wall wasn't smooth, offering plenty of places to put his hands and feet, but it was made into a major event by the injuries he had sustained. Slowly and cautiously he willed himself to the top, reaching out with a trembling hand for Mehya. She came as soon as she realized what she was seeing and pulled him over the edge to be greeted by yet another rough landing as he crumbled over the side.

"She didn't kill you!" The girl whispered, not wanting to be heard in case Lornamair was still in the area.

"Nope," said Ben hoarsely, partly wishing that she had.

"I wish there was something I could do for you," she said as she looked him over. She knelt beside him and used her gown to wipe most of the blood and dirt from his face while she cradled his head in her arms.

"Just…give me a few minutes." He had to fight the words out; breathing was becoming a difficult chore. "Do you know how many others like you there are here?"

"Prisoners?" Said Mehya. "I think six, but I can't be sure. It has been a long time since I heard their cries; she punishes us for making noise. I think there are wells like this one around the edge of the island, and women chained to each."

"But you've never had contact with any of them?" Ben pressed.

"No, why?" Asked Mehya, her dark eyes reflecting confusion.

"I was hoping that maybe you could tell me something about what you all had in common," Ben began. "I know what I've heard—that her only purpose is to ruin happy relationships—but I've been to Luna myself and I know that yours weren't the only happy relationships in town. Have you ever thought about why she chose you?"

"…No," Mehya replied, "and it doesn't matter. I'm here."

"And you've never seen anyone else here? Anyone not a prisoner?"

"No," she said again.

Ben nodded, and thought for a moment. "Something you said earlier struck me while I was in that well," he continued. "You said that I couldn't have found my way here on my own. No one could have. And you're right." Mehya looked confused, but Ben was no longer talking to her. He was getting closer... "People have been coming out here, trying to take back what she steals, for years." He looked again at Mehya. "Are you aware of anyone ever making it back?"

"No," she answered. "Not ever in the long history of Luna."

"Me, neither," said Ben, shaking his head. "But the guy who sent me out here knew exactly how to tell me to get here, without so much as a map of the ocean. How is that possible if no one has ever made it out of here alive? This isn't the only island off of the coast. How could he know which one was right?"

Mehya was beginning to get the picture. "So someone has been directing people here? Who? What does that mean?"

"It means that he's been here," Ben breathed, "and remembers the way." It was a revelation, but it was not everything. He was close to the vital piece of information he needed to make sense of it all, but it was still out of reach. It would have to stay there, too, for the time being.

Ben leaned forward, not willing to wait any longer, and got up with a hidden reserve of strength known only to heroes.

Mehya reached out and took his wrist in her hands, looking up at him with pleading eyes. "I'm afraid for you," she whispered. "She does not forgive, and she feels no pity."

"It's okay," he said. "She thinks I'm dead, so hopefully the rest of the trip will be easier. Like I said, I'll be back for you." He went back into the forest to finish his journey, leaving the girl hopeful.

When Ben finally cleared the last stretch of forest he was immensely grateful to have room to spread out. There was no forest at all from where he stood to what he presumed to be the cliff that he and Chris had been looking up at when they arrived, about a hundred and fifty feet ahead. It seemed like the trees had intentionally stopped growing and for reasons unknown left the tip of the island bare. It was the only part of it that leveled off, allowing for natural balance to at last prevail. He was once again thankful for the clear night and the full moon as he looked around at the clearing. The only thing worth noting to him was the man-made opening in the side of the hill in the area off to the right. Ben knew for certain then that it was the same hill that dominated his view when he had arrived and had been looking at the island from the beach. Inside the opening he could see light—firelight, it seemed—and from the inside could be heard the faint sound of a woman crying. Ben's tired legs hoped that he had finally found what he had come for.

At that point he knew better than to trust what he heard on that island. His ears had only picked up one source of sound, so there was no guarantee that Lornamair was even in there. In fact, it had to be considered that she was standing somewhere close by, watching him, as she seemed to be so good at doing, from a place that he wasn't paying any attention to—and God knew how many pits were dug out there.

Unfortunately for Ben, he had no way to draw her out into the open even if that was the case. His only choice seemed to be to approach the den in the hill and be ready for anything—an ambush, a pitfall—anything. He looked at the ground between him and the Den; it looked solid enough, the dirt having been packed down over years and years by constant treading. Taking a deep breath and making sure that he never let his eyes rest in the same place for more than a moment, Ben started to move toward the Den.

As he got closer he started to pick up another voice, just barely audible over the crying and incoherent from where he was. Suddenly there was the unmistakable sound of a hand being swung across someone's face and Ben decided that Lornamair was indeed inside. He crept up to the entrance and peered in from the side, and from there it was much easier to see and hear what was going on.

The fluttering firelight was being produced by a makeshift torch that was sitting on the wall on the side of the tiny room opposite the two women who were face to face on the other side. It made facial features hard to make out, but Ben didn't need fluorescent lighting to recognize his wife. Her arms were wrapped around behind her and bound with cloth behind a log that stood on its end and leaned against the wall across from the torch. Her head was lowered and her body was shaking with her soft sobs as she listened to Lornamair's scolding.

The Den's interior was plain, except for one surprising feature—stacks and stacks of books lined most of the circular stone wall, books of all different ages and what looked like at least a dozen languages. Most of the English ones, Ben recognized. There, sprinkled in a stack full of paperbacks about astronomy, were Jonathan Swift, Edgar Alan Poe, and Rudyard Kipling. There were yellowed newspaper clippings exploding out of each stack at different heights, magazines, and several scrolls that came from God-knew-where and contained God-knew-what. There were leather bound volumes that looked downright ancient, their sheer size assuring their importance. Taken with the torchlight, the patchwork library had a very arcane feel.

"He came here to get you," Lornamair was saying, her head lowered with Lindsey's so that her captive knew that she was being stared at despite having her eyes closed. "Can you believe that?" Lindsey said nothing, but her sobs became more frequent. "You're crying more tonight than you have in the last eight months, Love," said Lornamair, with traces of mock sympathy in her voice. "I wonder why that is… it couldn't actually be grief, could it? No…" She grabbed a fistful of Lindsey's hair and jerked her head upright so that the two had no choice but to stare at each other. "You're crying because that man was your ticket off this island, aren't you? *Typical,*" she spat. "I don't expect you to blame yourself, my Dear, but you probab*nngg!*"

Her sentence was interrupted when Ben threw all of his weight into her from the side and drove her until they were both stopped by the unforgiving stone wall that made up the interior of the den, scattering books of all kinds in the process. Ben had the strongest bear hug on her that he had ever had on anything, and for a moment he thought that it could hold. When Lornamair reacted, though, it didn't have a chance. She spread her arms as though his weren't even there and shoved him away from her violently enough to make him stumble backwards and fall; the athleticism packed in that diminutive frame was unearthly. The rage in her eyes was frightening as she simply stood there and watched him scramble to his feet, ready for a fight.

"That's the first time in a long time that anyone has *dared* to touch me," she said, her voice low and threatening, her eyes wide and vengeful. Ben wasn't fazed by the shove or the hatred.

"It won't be the last if you don't let my wife go right now," he said.

"Be careful what you wish for," Lornamair hissed. "You should thank me for what I took from you."

"Thank you for what?" Ben asked rhetorically, feeling his own anger once again beginning to manifest. "You have no idea what life has been like for me. Nothing about it has felt right since then. Let her go." Lornamair looked over at Lindsey, seething with anger.

"You hear that? His life hasn't been right since he lost you. Tell him how that makes you feel." Lindsey hadn't been able to do anything but stare at Ben from the moment he had made his presence known, and in her face he saw a mixture of relief and fear that he found confusing. As Lornamair took a step toward Lindsey her open hand shot up and across Lindsey's face with violent decisiveness. If Ben hadn't been able to see it he would have sworn that someone had just cracked a bullwhip. *"Tell him!"* She ordered. Lindsey's answer was barely more than a whimper.

"Appreciated," she said.

"Right," Lornamair said slowly, her face a mask of mock concern. "And how do we show our appreciation for the people who love us?" Tears were streaming down Lindsey's dirty face as she answered.

"By loving them back," she said, forcing the words through sobs. Ben got the feeling that this dialogue had already happened between the two of them many times, and he had no intention of letting Lindsey suffer through it anymore.

"This is sick, and pointless," Ben stated, his voice hollow.

"I assure you, it has a point." Lornamair had practically interrupted him, her voice a low and ferocious growl.

"What could *possibly* be the point?!" Ben shouted, unmindful of Lornamair's hostile temper. Lornamair, obviously unaccustomed to argument, simply kept letting her eyes burn paths through Ben's soul as he continued, undaunted. "Kidnapping? Torture? Murder? You expect me to believe that there's something noble to all that? You want me to believe that tying my wife to a log and slapping the living hell out of her is part of some elaborate scheme to make her a better person? *You want me to believe that jealousy isn't your only motive?! Save it!"*

Lornamair, who had been glaring sidelong at Ben, slowly pivoted on the balls of her feet and faced him squarely, maintaining that piercing eye contact that was sure to haunt his dreams for a long, long time as she did so. She began to take very slow, very elegant steps toward Ben, gradually closing the distance between them like a vampire who had hypnotized its prey. Her approach, which, under different circumstances, could have been misinterpreted as erotic, was instead a promise of pain at best, death at worst. It occurred to Ben that maybe he shouldn't have raised his voice. He hadn't intended to run, but the sight of her easing her way over to him like a femme fatale ready to cut him to pieces made him instinctively flatten himself against the stacks of books at his back. When Lornamair finally stopped, her face no more than a foot from his, he broke into a cold sweat. *I'm going to get buried out here,* he thought, once again captivated by her icy, deep stare.

Lornamair stared up at him for an eternity, never blinking once, underlining and re-underlining her unspoken warning about his tone of voice. When she was sure that the message had been delivered, her answer to his accusations came out silky and drenched in tolerance. "You believe whatever you're told."

Ben's mind, meanwhile, had calculated his probability of survival, and he decided a dead man had nothing to lose by speaking his mind. When he spoke, though, his volume had fallen quite a few notches. "I know what I see. I see innocent people becoming terrified of love because of a grudge that should have been put to bed long ago. I see a bitter and lonely—whatever you are—unwilling to let the past be the past. I see my wife, who I have missed dearly for two years, in need of medical attention." At some point during this last statement, Ben was no longer afraid. His nerves had calmed, and he was able to return Lornamair's stare confidently for the first time all night. "I see people in chains being told to apologize for something that no human being should ever be sorry for."

Lornamair inched closer, but Ben stood firm, relaxing away from the wall a bit to take back some of his personal space, which she didn't relinquish. "And what might that be?" She asked, unimpressed by his show of courage.

"...Love," Ben answered. "No one should apologize for love."

For the first time since they had met, Lornamair smiled, but it never reached her eyes. "Is that what she told you?" She asked rhetorically, nodding as though she had been expecting it. Ben, uncertain, said nothing. Lornamair reached (painstakingly slowly, of course) for something out of his peripheral vision, and brought back the hunting knife that she had taken from him earlier. Lindsey, who had been watching the whole exchange, began to cry again, bringing a barely discernible touch of euphoria to Lornamair's eyes as she pressed the blade against Ben's throat. "You're a fool," she reminded him with a whisper. "You're a fool for assuming that they don't deserve it."

Ben closed his eyes and prepared for death, but it never came. Instead of feeling cold steel cut through his neck, he felt Lornamair pull back and then slip the knife into the empty sheath that hung at his belt. Ben didn't open his eyes; a big part of him didn't believe he was still alive. The next voice he heard, though, didn't belong to something from the afterlife—it belonged to Lornamair.

"People like Mehya thrive on telling you half of the truth," she said. "And only in a world as fickle and self-indulgent as yours can you say that what any of them felt was love." Ben opened his eyes as she stepped away, returning her attention to Lindsey. She put a hand under Lindsey's chin and lifted her head, searching her captive's eyes for something known only to her. "There's no chance you realize how lucky you are," she said quietly.

All things aside, and with the threat of having his throat cut gone, Ben decided that he was done with half of the truth. "If Mehya only told me half of the truth," he asked, "what's the other half?"

"Curious, all of a sudden?" The question came out sounding uncharacteristically conversational. "I didn't take her because she got married, or even because she claimed to be in love. I took her because she was an impostor. She was unfaithful."

Ben digested her claim, and then countered. "Mehya told me you did this because you didn't want anyone to be happy."

"Of course she did," said Lornamair, as if Ben had just told her that water was wet. Her face softened after a pause, and she said, "I don't expect you to believe me."

Ben's response was resolute. "It's impossible to know who to believe, so I won't waste my time trying to figure it out. It doesn't matter." He remembered that he had come here to free Lornamair's prisoners, and he didn't feel like he was making any progress. At the same time, it was evident that she couldn't be forced. Still, it couldn't hurt to get things back on topic. "Please just let everyone go."

"Now it's *everyone* you want freed," Lornamair observed, amused the way that cats were amused when the mouse made a break for it. "Being a bit presumptuous, aren't you? For all you know, they're here because they've killed people."

"But they're not," Ben answered, his voice betraying his fatigue.

"Not quite, no," Lornamair said. "But close, depending on your point of view. They're all here for the same reason."

It took a moment for Ben to get his head around what she was saying. "You mean they all cheated on their husbands?" Lornamair nodded, looking at him intently. Something was about to happen; her demeanor had changed. Ben couldn't quite identify her expression, but if he hadn't known better he might have thought she looked... worried. "How could you possibly know that?" He pressed. "Were you the lover in each case?"

Lornamair didn't appreciate his incredulity, or the mockery in his tone. But something in his questions had stung, if only a little; her face had gone from worried to sad. "I can't explain what I am," she said softly. "But I can feel it, as surely as you feel tired or hungry, when love is disrupted. It's part of what I am."

"Now who's being presumptuous?" Ben fired back. "How can you be sure that that's what you're feeling?"

"How can you be sure when you need to go to sleep?" She replied. "Feelings that are alien to me are natural for you. Feelings that you can't understand are natural for me."

It would be a huge leap of faith to believe what he was being told. But, then, hadn't Lornamair's very existence defied logic when he first heard her story? Maybe it wasn't such a stretch, then, that everyone she had taken—

Ben's blood froze the way it had the first time he had seen Lornamair, that chilling feeling that started at the base of the spine and rushed its way up to the head, shattering his train of thought. His eyes found Lindsey. *"Everyone* you've taken has...?" He trailed off, finally seeing what implications the island dweller's story was making. Lindsey was hanging her head, unwilling to look at her husband. Despite being exhausted, his heartbeat quickened. "I won't believe it unless I hear it," he said flatly, willing himself to certainty that the words would never come.

"Why did you have to be so persistent?" Lornamair asked, suddenly sympathetic. "Why couldn't you have just died?" Ben wasn't sure whether or not she was actually speaking to him or just talking to herself, but to be on the safe side he answered her question.

"I came here for a reason," he said, pointing at Lindsey with an unsteady hand and trying to remember what, exactly, the reason was.

"That's very noble," Lornamair said quietly. She then bristled and Ben saw the return of the murderous nymph with which he had been acquainted. Her expression was hateful, and, as he had been told, completely without pity. "You want to take her with you? That's a request easily enough granted." She turned back to Lindsey. "You know what you have to do," she told her. Lindsey looked away from Ben and shook her head, prompting Lornamair to laugh lightly, but bitterly. "This man has come all this way, *faced death* to find you, and you *still* don't want to come clean?" Her voice was almost hopeless, and definitely exasperated. "Then you stay here with me." It was Lindsey's turn to look hateful as she lifted her head and stared at her captor with burning eyes, but Lornamair's will didn't budge. She looked back at Lindsey with a very stern, parental face and said, "Don't you think he's earned some honesty?"

When Lindsey looked at Ben, he was immobilized, and time was temporarily not a part of his universe. What was about to happen was simply not possible. The very thought of it was too much for him to even comprehend. Even so, the impending moment was a tidal wave headed toward the shore of his sanity—inevitable and unavoidable, no matter how many times he might try to ignore its approach.

"Tell him why you're here," Lornamair ordered, and again Lindsey's eyes welled up with tears.

Ben's nails were digging into his palms, making his knuckles white and the veins in his arms strained. As the moment of truth inched closer, he tried meekly to postpone its arrival. "Don't say it," he whimpered, pleading with his wife and beginning to choke back tears of his own. "Please don't say it. *You can't say it. You didn't... You didn't...*" His eyes were closed and his head was shaking, his mouth grimacing with the stress of keeping his emotions within himself. Before Lindsey had said anything, the wave had broken.

When the words finally came, Ben almost regretted making the trip. "I'm here because I was unfaithful."

"You're making her say that!" Ben screamed at Lornamair, his emotional floodgates now broken. *"You jealous little **demon**, you're making her! Why should I believe a thing you're say—"*

*"You have no reason **not** to believe me, save that you were stupid enough to carry all your foolish and misguided hopes here with you!"* Lornamair shrieked, her temper lost and momentarily irretrievable. *"You come to my home to kill me because someone tells you I am evil, and you ask no questions!"* Even delirious with anger and hurt, Ben didn't take it lightly when he noticed that Lornamair was crying. ***"But I am not evil!"*** She screamed, though not in Ben's direction. She had literally backed herself into a corner of the Den and lowered herself onto her haunches, rocking as she manically ran her hands through her colorful mane of hair. ***"I am not evil!"*** She cried again, her tears kicking up dust from the floor as they landed. Ben could only watch,

stunned and fascinated, as she tried to collect herself, his own rage startled away by her display of all-too-human emotion. Lornamair looked up at him with wet, desperate eyes and reiterated her claim in a tiny wail that was starving for a trusting ear. *"I'm not evil."*

Ben's mind went in too many directions at once. It made enough sense that Lornamair, in all her hatred and jealousy, would make Lindsey say something like that for the sake of making Ben doubt whether or not he actually wanted his wife back. It was also possible that she was made to say it just to screw with Ben's head. And even if it *was* true, then which was more important—the fact that he had finally found his wife after two years of emotional desolation or the fact that he might have been misled as to why she disappeared in the first place? Should he be relieved that he was finally reunited with his love or devastated by the revelation that the love he thought they had was only a dream all along? Either way, Ben felt that undeniable alarm in his mind that went off when things didn't add up. Why would Lornamair bother with manipulation when she could just as easily kill him and keep Lindsey there as long as she liked? If jealousy was really her only motive, she wouldn't have much of a reason to deceive anyone but herself about why she did what she did. Only one thing was clear—despite what he wanted to think, he needed to figure out what to believe before doing anything else. He addressed Lindsey while Lornamair continued to get herself together.

"With who?" He asked with deliberate and strained calmness, bracing himself for the worst—which he got. Lindsey looked away a little and muttered something inaudible at the floor. Ben was about to explain how unacceptable an answer like that was when Lornamair saved him the trouble.

"It's the one you came here with," she said, wiping her eyes dry and sounding fed up with the lack of forthcoming. Her breakdown was already a distant memory, gone as quickly as a dead leaf in a typhoon, like every other feeling she seemed to experience.

There are moments among couples during which absolute truth is communicated without the assistance of any words whatsoever. When one knows another well enough, one becomes accustomed to the subtle messages sent through habits and body language and can perceive things being said that no one else perceives. It was Lindsey's unwillingness to make eye contact that erased all doubt from Ben's heart and mind; it was the bond they had formed in the past that informed him of the truth of things. Immediately he felt that same cold, desperate feeling he had experienced when his wife had first disappeared—the fear of losing a loved one and the reflexive denial of the loss.

"How long?" Ben pressed, his voice faltering. Lindsey now closed her eyes and her voice was barely audible.

"Since before we were married." That last bit of news cut Ben deeper than he had ever been cut, and Lornamair, who had stood up and been watching the exchange, winced when Lindsey delivered it, keeping her eyes on Ben. It had been a long night for Ben's legs; they had been on the move since he arrived, cut by thorns, pierced by deathtraps, and banged against rocks, and they had nothing left. He fell to his knees, worn out and unable to look away from Lindsey, who wouldn't return his pleading, wounded gaze.

"Then why did we *get* married?" He asked weakly, all the wrong emotions making themselves present at this time that he had imagined would be so happy for him. Lindsey said nothing and Lornamair simply continued to watch him. It was evident to Ben in that moment that while she may have had a reason for ruining (and ending) so many lives, it was not the reason he had been given by others. If what they had said was true, he would have been dead long ago and the entire reunion would never have taken place. In those vibrant green eyes of hers, which just a short while ago had reflected nothing but hatred and contempt, Ben saw something that he never would have thought possible—concern. "Why wasn't I good enough? What did I do wrong?" He was asking Lornamair every bit as much as he was asking Lindsey, and he didn't care who answered. "Why couldn't you tell me?" The questions kept coming, but Lindsey refused to speak again. But if Ben could get nothing else, he at least wanted to know why it had all been kept from him. "Why couldn't you tell me?" He asked again.

"Shame, I imagine," said Lornamair, and Ben knew that she was probably on to something. Still, it only seemed fair that Lindsey should have to say it. Fair, however, didn't seem to be part of this exercise.

Ben's eyes stayed on his wife. He couldn't have known then that their eyes had already met for the last time, but Lindsey's stubborn unwillingness to return his gaze had started to paint the picture for him. His expression—and heart—went from unspeakably hurt to mildly disgusted in the same way that day turns to night.

"What now?" He asked Lornamair darkly, once he had accepted Lindsey's silence.

"Use the rocks, not the beach," she told him. Ben was lost, and his face must have given it away, because Lornamair took the liberty of explaining herself. "When you jump, don't jump onto the beach; there's no guarantee it will kill you. Walk around to where it ends and dive into the rocks instead."

"Lady," he said tiredly, "if you think I'm going to save you the trouble of a fight, you got me all wrong."

"I'm not going to *make* you," she said, her brow furrowed, "but it's the easiest way to go. If you want to die painfully, by all means, I won't stop you."

"I don't want to die at all," Ben said.

"…Oh."

Ben was mystified, but too tired to try and understand her logic. The important thing was that it didn't seem as though she wanted to kill him anymore—what had changed, though, he didn't quite know. "So…are we done here?" He asked.

"Yes, we are," came the half-unexpected reply.

"I'm afraid I don't quite understand," Ben sighed, long ago tired of the entire episode. "Why have you not killed me?"

"I was only trying to save you from…this," she said, waving a hand in Lindsey's general direction. Ben was dumbfounded, but again, too tired to really think. And when you got right down to it, he knew better than to look a gift horse in the mouth.

He gathered what strength he had left in his legs and stood again. "I'm going outside," he said to Lornamair. "Please have her untied by the time I get back in." Lornamair made no move in response and Ben left without needing one.

He went out and walked stiffly toward the edge of the drop off, stopping a good thirty feet from its edge when the exhaustion in his legs again caught up with him. He sat down awkwardly, feeling all the aches and pains of the evening at once, looking up at the starry sky for some kind of justification, finding none. He sat there, more than content to be alone for the moment, turning things over in his mind. It all seemed so unfair. All the worry that had set in when Lindsey had disappeared, the two years of depression and sadness that followed, and the painful and dangerous trek through the island hardly seemed worth the trouble just to find out that he had never really been loved in the first place. But then again, who knew? Love could be a fickle thing. Maybe his expectations were just too high.

Dawn

The sky over the endless horizon was crimson when he heard the sound of soft footsteps approach from behind. He wasn't yet in the mood to hash anything out with Lindsey, so he was actually relieved when he saw that it was Lornamair who had come out to see him. She sat down gracefully just a few feet away, her legs stretched out and crossed at the ankles. Leaning back on her hands, she never took her eyes off of the horizon as she spoke to Ben.

"I haven't untied her yet. Will you make it?" She asked. Ben looked wearily at the woman who had tried to kill him three times over the last eight hours, wondering whether or not he had heard correctly.

"Why are you so concerned all of a sudden?"

"I told you, I just didn't want you to find out," she said apologetically. Ben was as thunderstruck as a man in his condition could be.

"Is *that* what all the violence was about?" Lornamair nodded. "You thought it would be better to kill me than to let me know the truth about what she had been doing?" She nodded again. "Why?" Ben asked, her rationality totally beyond his comprehension.

"I remember what it felt like when I found out," Lornamair began. "It's something I've had to live

97

with all this time here, and if it had been up to me I never would have known." She shook her head and her emerald green eyes seemed even more distant than they had before. "It was too much to live with. Loving him had been my life, and that life was taken away from me. That love had been my reason for living."

"Then out of curiosity," Ben said, "why haven't you killed *yourself?* Why take all these other people with you?"

"I tried dozens of times, long ago," she answered. "But I gave up. Besides, I only take people when they've been unfaithful; the ones who die are the ones who come after them. Half of them I kill trying to keep them from being hurt, and the other half kill themselves after they find out what you found out." Ben thought of the skeleton in the well, and then put two and two together.

"That's why you expected me to jump after we talked."

"You're the first one who has chosen not to," she confessed.

"That seems a little extreme, doesn't it? Do the people here really have such a hard time dealing with this?" Lornamair smiled a little before answering.

Luna is a simple place, Ben," she explained. "For most of the people there, love is life's destination. There's nothing for them there to help them move on. When their love dies, often times they aren't far behind. But not knowing that kind of truth allows most of them to carry that love with them. When life itself has been love, losing that is worse than dying." Ben was filled with sympathy of his own as he recalled what the villagers in Luna had told him about

Lornamair. "And you weren't in great condition when you found out, either."

"Not ready to *die,* though," he argued.

"Apparently not. Yet how close to death were you already, I wonder? How many years of your life have you thrown away on that whore in there, years that you can never get back? How much time have you wasted, dead to the world, miserable and unable to move on?"

"Listen to who's telling me about moving on," Ben chided. "But you're right. So why haven't *you* done it?"

"Done what?"

"Moved on."

"Sense of duty," Lornamair said. "I told you, I can feel it when love is abused. I can't explain it any more than I can explain exactly where I came from, but the feeling is almost unbearable. It's like reliving the first time, again and again. And then I'm afraid for the faithful one. They never handle it well when they find out. So I do my best to keep them from finding out, and I remove their partners from their lives. I know it scares them, and I know they curse me for it, but it's the best thing for them whether they realize it or not; they deserve better. I was in Luna the day you and your wife arrived, and I felt your corrupted bond immediately. *You* deserve better." She looked down at the knives at Ben's belt. "I know whose those belong to," she said. "And *he* deserved better, too. Good men deserve good women, and vice versa. Not childish, ungrateful *whores* masquerading as loving companions."

"Even if that's what they are," Ben countered, "that's no justification for captivity and torture."

"That may be," Lornamair admitted, "but I still won't tolerate people taking someone's love for granted—nor will I as long as I breathe. Like I said, I remember what it felt like. Besides, there's no justification for that, either."

"They told me you only ruined happy relationships," he said.

"They were telling the truth. Wasn't yours?" She pointed out. Ben pursed his lips and nodded slowly, fighting back a wave of tears. "They're only happy because of the lies," she finished.

"Yes, it was happy," he said. "At least for one of us."

"Oh, it was for both of you," Lornamair assured sourly. "That seems to be what having a lot of money does, I'm afraid."

"She said that she married me for my money?"

"They tell me everything," she said with sinister satisfaction. "The hard part is getting them to admit it to themselves first. I spend many, many nights talking to them, trying to understand what drives them to stray. I try to understand how love becomes warped and corrupted, and how they were ever able to sleep at night knowing that they behaved like faithless little harlots." She paused, calmed herself, and then continued. "I think that maybe, if I understood these things, I would understand what happened to me."

Ben had almost forgotten how it all began. "Do you still love your husband?" He wanted to know.

Lornamair turned her head to look at him and her eyes were cold when she answered with a question of her own. "Why else would I hate him?"

Ben considered her answer and decided that it made a lot of unexpected sense, which was much more than he could say for the rest of the situation.

"There's a lot of this that doesn't make sense, you know," he said.

"Oh?" Lornamair asked, her gaze toward the sunrise now disinterested. "Is there something about your wife's hedonism you don't understand?"

"I don't mean morally," Ben said, ignoring the insensitive joke. "I mean...have you ever brought any men out here?"

"No," she said.

"Don't you think that's a bit strange, that in all this time you never found a man cheating on a wife?"

"I think it's irrelevant," she said. "Why should I care who's doing what? It has to stop."

"Right, I get that," Ben continued. "But isn't it odd that all the offenders have been women? Men aren't any less susceptible to promiscuity than women are."

"I've never felt the presence of an unfaithful man," she responded. "If I had, I would have taken him."

"Do you really believe that among so many unfaithful women, there wasn't one man to find? And that isn't the only problem," Ben said. "You said yourself that for the people in Luna, love is life's destination. How, then, are there so many cheaters out there to begin with?" Lornamair either wasn't following, or didn't care. "People there have put so much stock in love that they're ready to die when it goes wrong," he went on. "And until Lindsey, you had only taken natives, right?"

"That's right," she said. "Although it would probably be different if Luna had more visitors than it does."

"Never mind that," Ben told her. "You're telling me that in the same culture, in the same society, half of the people in it care so much about love that they're willing to die for it, while the other half cares so little that they're willing to cheat despite knowing that *you're* out here watching? *And* that the dividing line falls squarely between men and women? Even if it didn't, I've seen enough of Luna to know that it doesn't have enough contact with the outside world to be that freakishly diverse among such a small group of people. The place is just too primitive."

"I see your point," said Lornamair. "What I don't see is what exactly you're trying to figure out."

"Where are the men?" Ben asked.

"It's very possible that they don't live in Luna, and are too far away for me to feel," Lornamair ventured. "I don't know all of the comings and goings of Luna, and I can't feel the whole *world.*"

"Even if that was true, which I doubt," Ben asserted, "that doesn't explain why the women of Luna are so willing to have affairs; they still know you're out here, and they've grown up feeling the same way about love as everyone else there. It just doesn't make a bit of sense."

"You're right," she said. "It doesn't. Fortunately for me, I'm not burdened with your driving curiosity."

"I'm still trying to make sense of what I'm doing here in the first place," Ben told her. "It feels like I was *sent* here more than it feels like I was *pointed* here."

"Well, you have plenty of time to figure it out," Lornamair said. "Those wounds are going to need time to heal."

"It'll have to wait," Ben said. "I have someone waiting for me on the beach; I need to let him know

I'm okay, and I'll rest up after we've all gotten home."

"The man who came here with you is Lindsey's lover," Lornamair recalled. "I could feel his nerves the moment you showed up. He was nervous enough to make the trees shudder."

"That seems to be the case, yes," Ben sighed. "It'll make for a pretty awkward boat ride, huh?"

"Ben?"

"Yes?"

"He isn't down there."

For a second, Ben thought about asking her what she meant, but then decided that she could only mean one thing. A more relevant question was probably in order. "Where is he?" He asked apprehensively.

"I don't know. Gone," Lornamair answered. She then nodded at the edge of the drop thirty feet in front of them. "Go see for yourself." When Ben got to the edge after a slow and painful crawl (it hurt too much to stand and walk), he saw that she was speaking the truth. He was overlooking the same part of the beach that he and Chris had pulled up on. The footprints he had made when he had started running were clearly visible in the sand, and when he traced them back with his eyes he saw that they seemed to originate from the water; there was no boat in sight. Immediately Ben thought with horror that he knew the reason.

"Christ, did you *kill* him?!" He shouted, looking back at her over his shoulder. He looked again down at the beach, then back to Lornamair. "Did you at least save the boat?! How am I supposed to get out of here?!"

"Don't panic, I can take you back," she called to him. "And I had nothing to do with that. I watched him take the boat and leave as soon as you were out of sight last night."

Ben kept staring at the shoreline, bewildered. "Why?" He wasn't posing the question to anyone, but Lornamair took a thoroughly educated guess anyway.

"He must have known that you might find out Lindsey's little secret," she said. "He was probably worried about the repercussions." Ben thought about it as he made the crawl back to where he had been sitting.

"He didn't even believe there was anyone here," he said, shaking his head and still having trouble knowing what to think. "He left as soon as I was out of sight?" Lornamair nodded. "...He *left* me here?" The more he thought about it, the angrier he got. *"Why?"* Knowing that Ben was starting to understand what Chris's departure meant, Lornamair declined to comment. Soon enough Ben decided that the reason wasn't really important anyway. "Well, it's just one thing after another, isn't it?" He said, the words spoken through angry laughter that underlined his frustration. It was only moments, though, before the anger disappeared and was replaced by a sense of defeat that felt like the killing blow at the end of a long series of fatal strikes. "He left me here to die."

"It would seem so," Lornamair said solemnly.

"He didn't even have the decency to face me."

"He isn't the first coward who didn't want to take responsibility for what he did," she said. "You're on an island full of them right now. It really isn't that stunning; people regret impulse all the time. They're ashamed of it once that passionate rush disappears and all they have to show for it is potentially incriminating evidence and the knowledge that they betrayed a friend. Can you blame them for not wanting to face it?"

"Yeah, I think I can," Ben said flatly, his anger having waned into new, unexplored levels of disappointment. He finally let his body relax and lay flat on his back, eyes open but staring at nothing in particular. "God, I'm tired."

"I told you, you can stay here," Lornamair reminded him. "Stay as long as you need to."

"Thank you," Ben said sincerely, thinking about how strange it was that he would be thanking her for anything given the events that had transpired overnight. "I didn't believe you at first, but you're right." Lornamair looked at him with mild interest, her eyes asking him to explain what he meant. "You're not evil," Ben said. The Solitary One afforded him a slight, soft smile.

"Thank you," she whispered back.

"But you have to admit, you've done some fairly extreme things," Ben added.

"I've done nothing that I would consider a mistake," Lornamair shot back, her response quick and firm.

"Isn't it about time to put this thing to bed?" He asked, thinking of the promise he had made to Mehya. It wasn't going to be an easy argument, but at least it was going to be an argument, and not a fight to the death, as he had been anticipating.

"No, it isn't," she snapped defiantly. "I'll put it to bed when Luna is faithful." As she looked at Ben, recognition found its way into her eyes. "Ah, yes," she breathed. "I had forgotten—you wanted me to let *everyone* go, didn't you?" Ben simply nodded, knowing he would have to choose his words carefully when he spoke. "And what, then, would you have me do?" She asked, her smile growing wider as though expecting Ben to deliver the punch line he was cooking up any second. "Retire, I suppose? From kidnapping and torture?" Ben felt as though he might as well have proposed that she rewind time itself to accommodate him, for all the consideration she was evidently giving his idea. "I like kidnapping and torture," she finished, with a steady stare. "And those are your words, not mine."

"Well what would you call it?" He knew the answer before he finished the question.

"Justice," they said in unison, Lornamair holding her gaze steady and Ben throwing his hands up in mild exasperation.

"Am I really asking that much?" He asked, unable to discern how many of her words were spoken just to give him a hard time. For someone so nakedly honest and unapologetic, she had a firm grasp on sarcasm and a knack for implication. It made it hard to tell how much of what she said, she actually meant, or if she just said it because it made her laugh inside. Ben then wondered what her laughter sounded like.

"You're asking a world," she said. *"My* world. You're asking me to change what I am. I don't actually enjoy being alone all the time, but I have a purpose. You're asking me to throw that purpose away. What am I supposed to do when my reason for living is gone?"

"The same thing I have to do," Ben answered. "Find another."

The incredulous smile that Lornamair had been wearing slowly faded as it gradually dawned on her that Ben's punch line was never coming. "And what of the faithless?" She asked, taking the conversation seriously for the first time.

"What of them?" Ben replied.

"Am I to knowingly allow their hedonism and lust to corrupt the only thing that I—"

"You aren't changing anything," Ben interrupted. "You must know that. There's a big world out there, and Luna doesn't count for very much of it. These things that you hate happen all over the world, every day, and nothing you've done has taken a single step toward changing it. The rest of the world has almost no idea Luna is even there. You're affecting practically nothing, and we both know it."

Lornamair's pretty face was now firmly stuck in a frown, her momentary silence speaking volumes about how much Ben's words had hurt. He understood then that, despite everything that had been said, he was dealing with someone who was ultimately very fragile. He felt a great swell of pity when it came to him that through it all, Lindsey hadn't been the one who needed saving.

"I fail to see how that is a good reason to neglect the ones that I *can* affect," she said softly. "You say that I can't reach the entire world, and maybe you're right. But I don't think that that should stop me from doing what good I can."

"But you haven't *done* any good in Luna," Ben said gently, reminding himself to stay conscious of her feelings. "Have you ever stopped taking people? Has the entirety of Luna stayed faithful because of your intervention? They're still human, and they're going to continue to do these things forever if what you've done hasn't been enough to stop them already. At the end of the day, all you're doing is scaring them, and speaking from experience, everyone can do well enough without that."

Lornamair drew her knees up to her chest and hugged her legs, her eyes having resumed their search for nothing on the horizon. Ben, who had been watching her and trying to determine if any of his words were finding purchase, now tried to follow her stare out across the sea to a specific location, but saw nothing notable. If she was, in fact, searching for something, it was more than likely that she was looking for it on the inside. Her silence allowed him time to wonder what it could be. A better reason to keep her captives, maybe? What it would be like to find a new life? Or maybe there were no questions in there at all. Maybe their talking had led her to a distant and regretful past, haunted by memories and feelings that were now no more than collateral damage in an internal war between love and hate, emotion and duty. Or... was it possible that she was thinking about conceding? The further Ben got into making his case, the more he sensed that Lornamair was scrambling to justify what her life had become. He had never seen her show fear, but something told him that she was, indeed, beginning to tremble inside. Whether that was a good thing or a bad thing had yet to be seen. "All those books, and there's nothing in there about me," she said quietly.

"I understand, as hard as all this has been for me, that I have no idea how to relate to what I'm asking you to do," Ben admitted. "I have no idea what it's like to exist for so long, to devote myself so entirely to one purpose, and then consider throwing that purpose away. But just because it's the only purpose you've ever known doesn't mean that there isn't a better alternative." Watching Lornamair stare vacantly out to sea yielded no information whatsoever about what she was thinking. Ben's confidence that he was getting anywhere with her was shaky at best, but there wasn't much left for him to say that he hadn't already said. "I think you should let them go."

Lornamair drew her eyes away from the horizon and fixed them on Ben. It was easy for him to notice that the frozen edge that usually accompanied those eyes was absent. "I think," she said, "that you've lost more blood than you realize. Your wounds need time to heal." She was dodging the issue, Ben knew, but that was a long way from a refusal. He considered his side of the argument an overwhelming success, even if she was going to need time to digest it.

Lornamair pulled her feet under her and stood fluidly. "Let me help you to somewhere more comfortable," she said. "There *are* actually places in the Den that you can occupy without being imprisoned."

As much as the idea of relaxation appealed to Ben, he had no desire to see Lindsey. Not yet, maybe not ever. He hadn't had the opportunity to stop and consider how much it actually mattered anymore. He had come to Lornamair's island to resurrect his marriage, but now, for the first time, he finally and truly believed it was over. Such an end to the relationship on which he had built his life made everything seem false and temporary and… and he had no desire to see Lindsey. "Is there somewhere else I could go?" He asked wearily.

Lornamair didn't need an explanation. She nodded and spoke gently, "I can set you up out here if you like, maybe against the wall of the Den. There's no wildlife here, and it would be easy to make you something soft to sleep on, I'm sure."

Ben stayed put while Lornamair set to work gathering leaves and stuffing them into a large, human-sized sack, undoubtedly homemade and probably not intended for the function it was about to perform. Once it was filled, however, Ben found that in his condition he couldn't distinguish between it and the world's softest feather mattress once he had lain down. Lornamair propped one end of the makeshift bed up against the side of the Den to prevent Ben from lying completely flat and backed away a few steps, admiring her work. "All set," she said, affording Ben a slight, soft smile.

"Thank you so much," Ben said, resting his head against the "pillow" and immediately beginning to drift away. As consciousness left him, he acknowledged that it was a good thing that Lornamair no longer wanted to kill him; there was no way he could stay awake and defend himself, even if she did.

Lornamair came forward and leaned in close, the way a mother tucked in a child at bedtime. "It's the least I can do," she said, her eyes soft and assuring. She stepped away from Ben, who had already left the waking world. For a few moments, she envied his ability to sleep—to lose track of the world and its cruelty must be a blissful ignorance indeed, even if only for a few hours. She felt a pang of regret at having put him through so much during his short time on the island. Unexpectedly, she realized that she liked Ben—if only everyone could be so committed. He had definitely earned his rest, and she felt obliged to leave him to it. She turned and walked toward the Den, her heart and mind heavy with alien thoughts and mostly unwelcome feelings. She didn't want to like Ben; she didn't want to listen to what he had to say. Anger was so much easier, so much less complicated, than the tangle of emotion that came with love or compassion. Even now it was undeniable how much simpler things would be if she hadn't let Ben survive his visit to her home, her sanctuary. Anger would never have had to make room for the twinges of doubt and whispers of a memory of a life that was about anything else that she now felt and heard. There would be no argument, no silly questioning of why things were the way they were or if they had to be. Anger was what she was, what she wanted to be, and it was *justified*. Without Ben there would be no doubt—there would be only anger, and things would be simpler.

Lornamair's typical glide had become a march in the short time it took her to reach the Den. She continued to storm quickly through the main room once inside, not offering Lindsey so much as a glance as she passed through. Self-preservation was not a force to be trifled with. Lornamair knew for an absolute certainty that her very presence thoroughly terrified Lindsey, and to catch her in a worse mood than usual must have been even less appealing. But that didn't stop the pathetic little wretch from asking about her ticket home.

Despite knowing that her captive didn't rate the slightest bit of acknowledgment, she couldn't help but feel her blood burn white hot when Lindsey asked meekly, "Where's my Ben?"

Lornamair didn't react; it was an audacious question, and the vermin had done nothing to deserve an explanation or even a response. It satisfied her to let her captive continue to tremble and wonder what was going on—to let her hope that she might leave after all, only to swat those hopes like annoying insects at a moment of her choosing. She was better than her prisoners—more sincere, more dedicated, more *feeling*. She had loved truly, and they had loved falsely. She had appreciated her life, and they had taken what they had for granted. That was what bothered her the most, she knew—the lack of appreciation. Lornamair would never understand why they let themselves be driven by such a superficial—though apparently insatiable—need to stray. There must have been something misplaced in the human mind—something that made her captives invariably turn to new things, places, and experiences for the solution to the problem of contentment, as if that solution was ever anywhere outside of themselves. As long as they were allowed to indulge in their every whim and impulse, they would always look in the wrong places for that answer.

But with her, they learned otherwise. When life was too easy, the heart and mind got bored and lazy. Trials were what brought the essential things back into focus, pain the only real method of awakening. Those who didn't appreciate love simply didn't deserve to have love, and love was only one of the things on the long list of luxuries that Lornamair took from them. She took their comfort, their security, their freedom. She broke their spirits, derailed their hopes, drained their will to live. After enough time with her they begged for the life they once took for granted, and for the man they had neglected in the meantime. By the time it was over, they all learned an unforgettable lesson about what really mattered. Who was Ben to suggest that she did no good...?

A subtle and unfamiliar voice disrupted her train of thought. *But it's never over, and what use is the lesson if you never let them go? When will they ever have the chance to apply it if you keep them until they die?*

Lornamair spun around in the near-perfect darkness of the Den's rear chamber, and again, trying to get a fix on the intruder. After a moment, it was apparent that there was none. Her eyes widened and darted back and forth, blindly. Her lips began to tremble and her breathing became erratic. She wasn't yet willing to accept what the only explanation could be—it had been the voice of doubt, and it had come from within her own mind. A pulse of panic chilled her body, then another. Her eyes snapped shut for as long as it took her head to twitch sharply, trying irrationally to shake the new and invasive thoughts out. The spasms kept an unsteady beat with the surges of panic. The walls of the Den were too close, too close. A thought of Ben flashed through her mind, and she cursed him repeatedly for his intrusion—not just into her psyche, but everywhere. She cursed his dedication, cursed his survival, cursed all the damned sense he had made. In that instant, everything was wrong. The confusion was agitating. The panic was overwhelming.

Her thoughts came in a hurried, single-file march. Anger—the answer was anger. It always was. She had to be true to herself…

<Who are you?>

She had to have faith in her purpose…

<The purpose is not thought out>

It had to be. There were reasons. Good ones. She couldn't remember what they had been at the moment, but it didn't matter. They had been there. They still were. She had to let the anger take her, lead her back to the right way. She had to kill something…

"I said, *where's my Ben?*"

Carried away with her own frenzied, ringing thoughts, Lornamair had forgotten that the Den remained silent until Lindsey's voice crashed its way through the racket in her head. It caused the voices to stop, and then some. The mental commotion ceased. The doubt was removed, and there was focus. Her exterior was once again like an undisturbed lake— one that was always just a degree short of boiling, and it never took much to raise the temperature.

The Bitter One couldn't believe what she was hearing. Was the prisoner *raising her voice?* Was she *making demands?!*

Lindsey's resolve vanished when Lornamair's small, but nevertheless terrifying, form materialized out of the shadows of the rear chamber. Her voice was smooth when she spoke, but as usual, her heart was betrayed by eyes that blazed with contempt. Every slow, deliberate step she took was a threat, each foot gracefully placed in front of the other in a straight line that stopped just short of making them promises. "He's yours now, is he?"

Lindsey fell back on her usual response, which was nothing. Lornamair's disgust rose a notch; this one had no fight in her. She never did. She had no conviction, didn't act according to right or wrong— only what she wanted. She despaired easily, and it took almost no effort to really frighten the girl. All the same, she had never in all her time there once admitted fault. True, she acknowledged what she had done, and she understood why she had been taken, but she had never seemed to quite let go of the idea that what she had done was excusable, or justified, or...whatever. She just hung her head, hating her captor, unwilling to be reasoned into any guilt at all— unwilling to accept responsibility.

Not this time. Lindsey still had much to learn. First of all, when Lornamair wanted eye contact, she got it. Lornamair cupped her chin in one hand and raised her head, making Lindsey look into her eyes— never cold, but always chilling. "You're ready to claim ownership now? I'm afraid it's a bit late, Darling." Lindsey's eyes began to well up, which only encouraged her tormentor. "You threw him away. And I should remind you," she purred, "that as long as he's on this island, he belongs to me—and so do you."

Much to Lornamair's satisfaction, Lindsey couldn't stay the ensuing flow of tears. She had caused Lindsey to break down emotionally countless times over the past two years, and it never got old. "But he came here to take me home," she sobbed.

"He came here on a fool's errand," Lornamair stated calmly, her gaze steady. "Even he sees that. He came because he thought you loved him."

"I *do* love him," Lindsey said fiercely.

"You love him for being your only chance of getting away from me," Lornamair hissed back. There was no doubt that Lindsey believed what coming out of her own mouth, but she was wrong. Like most people, she let herself be fooled by panic and hope into thinking, even feeling, things that weren't true. "But you're never getting away from me," she continued. "He doesn't want you anymore." Her eyes narrowed as she finished Lindsey's hopes off with one more quick slash of the tongue. "You're all mine."

This time, the breakdown was epic. It began unfiltered, with silence and a look of pure horror. Lornamair watched Lindsey's face intently, her mouth practically watering in anticipation. It would only be a few moments until the despair reached its peak, and she wanted to taste it when it got there. She watched as Lindsey, her dirty face wide-eyed and terror-stricken, began to shake her head in a fruitless attempt to deny the words and somehow force them back into her captor's mouth. It started slightly, but became more forceful with every uttering of what was, at the moment, the only word left in her vocabulary. "No. No. *No.* No, no, no, no, no, no, no no no no no no no—"

Lornamair couldn't have hidden her delight even if she had wanted to, which she didn't. For a split second she wondered if Lindsey could taste her excitement in the same way that Lornamair could taste sorrow, and then it didn't matter. The rush was coming. She let it wash everything else out of her mind entirely, welcoming the gripping feeling of someone else's panic and the nagging chill of their regret. Before she noticed, her breathing had become deep and passionate, the world around her disappearing as her eyes slipped shut. Each exhalation nearly became a laugh, her ecstasy so intense that beads of sweat were collecting on her entire body, grabbing her clothes and hair and holding them tight against her skin. It was almost time, she was almost there. Lindsey was rapidly reaching that exquisite point that lay in the time just after horrifically bad news completely sank in and just before survival instinct had the chance to interfere and downplay the hopelessness. It was the Moment of Undiluted Sorrow, and Lornamair had seen it countless times before. It was the moment at which people chose to end their own lives, the moment at which everything in the world was seen for what it actually was instead of gilded by hope, expectations, and self-delusions. It was the only perfectly true thing in her universe, and, for Lornamair, the observer, it came with so many other complimentary feelings.

She knew what Lindsey was experiencing, because she had once been there herself. She hadn't deserved it, but that was the best part about bringing so many others to it—it was justice.

The thought of the word made her body tense and quiver. She pressed in close to Lindsey and dreamily put her arms around her captive with no regard whatsoever for Lindsey's personal space. While Lornamair was losing herself in the moment, Lindsey's whimpering had become crying, which had escalated into sobbing, which was now only one step shy of screaming and just moments away from the lamenting wail that Lornamair knew was coming. It was truth incarnate, and there would be no stopping or hiding it. In fact, it was coming now.

Lindsey screamed, and it was beautiful.

Revelation

While sleeping, Ben found that he wasn't so fatigued that he couldn't dream. The world was calm, as was his mood. He was still on Lornamair's island, but knew somehow that he was alone there. The air was warm and comfortable, the only sound that of the breeze moving the treetops. As minutes passed, he felt himself being rocked to sleep by the gentle scene and lazily wondered what would happen if someone were to fall asleep while sleeping. What came next? Death? It might not be so bad, all things considered. Maybe he was there already.

A voice interrupted his daze. It was hard to make out what it was saying, because it wasn't saying anything. It was faint, perhaps distant, as though it was being carried across the sea and through the trees on the wind. It was laughter that he was hearing. It was full-scale and almost malicious, and in a voice that he felt as though he should recognize. As nice as the scenery was, he couldn't bring himself to be more than half-interested in anything. Who was that laughing? If he couldn't remember immediately, then it probably wasn't something worth remembering at all. He wasn't very funny, and probably wouldn't get the joke anyway. Were they laughing at him? He hadn't given anyone a reason to laugh at him.

They *were* laughing at him. Who *was* that? His sleeping mind became sharp and aware, and he stared intently at the swaying treetops, trying to put a name to the voice. It was someone he knew, and someone he didn't entirely trust. It was someone he had seen recently. The laughter grew louder. Ben looked around and saw that he was laying in the very bed that Lornamair had made for him. He tried to remember why he had been put there in the first place, and then he had it. It was Roger. Why was Roger laughing at him in a dream?

Because he knows something you don't, he thought to himself.

Ben's eyes snapped open and he found himself on his mattress, staring at the same world he had experienced in his dream. It looked to be about late morning—how long had he been out? A day? More? Or only a few hours? Come to think of it, how did he know he was even awake? He listened for Roger's mocking laughter, but there was none. He listened for sounds coming out of the Den, but again detected nothing. The island felt deserted. He tried to sit up, but found that his body was entirely too sore for such an ambitious undertaking. Everything had stiffened up after he had gotten off of his feet, and it felt as though it would be awhile before he could consider moving around easily again. His wounds had stopped throbbing, though—at least there was that.

His mind was in a much better condition. To feel rested felt strange indeed; it seemed a lifetime ago that he had gotten a sufficient amount of sleep. Not since the first time Lornamair had come to see him, in fact. Lornamair—what a strange case she had turned out to be. It was incredible how misunderstood it all was. Misunderstood by most, anyway. He had a feeling that there was one man out there who understood much more than he let on. What he couldn't fathom, though, was what motive Roger could possibly have had to send him out there to his likely death. There *was* the small chance that he would succeed, he supposed, in which case the assumption would be that Lornamair was dead and he could finally make his dream of building Luna up into a reality. Money was a master motivator, and there was certainly a lot of it in the picture. Ben hated to think that all of his trouble had been for money, but what else was there? It just seemed so cliché, so basic.

Ben's consciousness disappointed him. It was strange, but while he was sleeping he had felt as though he was more likely to come across answers than he was while awake. He felt as though his subconscious already knew whatever truth there might have been to the situation, and staying awake only kept him from it. There was always something in front of him, something that his waking mind was unable to see. Well, it wasn't as if he was in a position to go anywhere. Maybe answers would come in his dreams...

When exposed to the breeze sweeping in from the sea, nighttime on Lornamair's island could be chilly, but Mehya was used to it. What did it matter, anyway? Comfort was only an illusion inflicted upon those whose lives were cursed with happiness. They were destined to lose both, but the dream of many was to remain blissfully ignorant of this reality. Happiness, for many lives, was solely dependent on how successful each person was at constructing and maintaining these palatable illusions which convinced them of absurdities like "death is far away," and "to be warm is to be comfortable," and "to have companionship is to be happy." Mehya had no need for such bedtime stories; she knew now that death was very much a relative term, and its arrival didn't necessarily coincide with one's body ceasing to function. Mehya's body, for example, was in its prime—but life was not something she had experienced in a long time. With life came feelings, emotion, and experience, and she had all but forgotten hers. What was a chilly breeze, if not a faithful reminder to be wary of the illusion that was comfort? Others all over the world continued to let it pull their strings, and she envied them nothing.

At least, that's what she told herself. She liked to think that she had been purged of her desire for freedom, that she had truly abandoned hope and therefore had nothing left to lose, and by extension, nothing left to fear. These days, she only rarely felt those old twinges of longing, so complete was her alienation of life.

Ah, but what lay beneath the surface? The stranger's arrival had stirred many unwelcome feelings inside of her, only to make her discover that they weren't unwelcome at all. The first glint of hope in years had come with the lesson that there was a very real difference between letting desires go and burying them. She was a fox who had convinced herself that the grapes were probably sour anyway. The difference was, leaving the grapes there to hang hadn't been her decision. And, of course, she already knew what they tasted like, and they tasted like paradise—a paradise that was taken from her.

She wanted it back. Mehya sat on her rock, trying as hard as she could to will the stranger to victory. He had to succeed. If he didn't, it would likely be years before the next fool decided to challenge the island's queen. Involuntarily, she started to daydream about his success. She would tell him that she wanted to see the body. She wanted to see it so that she could spit on it and carve that condescending look (which would surely still be there) off of her face forever. Yes, and then she would throw it face down into a shallow well, where it would rot unceremoniously and be forgotten by everyone who would have been able to recognize it. No, she could do better—she would put it in a noose and heave it over the front of the island, so that anyone who got close enough would see it hanging and witness the consequences of her cruelty. Or maybe, when she and the stranger left the island, she would tie it up and drag it behind the boat, and all the hungry fish would take pieces out of it and by the time they got back to Luna she would finally look like the monster she really was. Mehya could laugh in her face and tell her that she was free. She could return every slap she had endured, every insult, every little torment that her torturer thought she deserved. She wouldn't be able to beat her lost time out of the witch's body, but she would try.

A dreamy smile had crept onto Mehya's face. Oh, it was going to be so nice, so overdue…

Then, just like the rest of her hopes and dreams, it all came crashing down as Lornamair emerged from the forest and burst back into her life. Mehya simply stared, dead-eyed, traumatized but feeling nothing at all. In a few seconds, reality was once again what it had always been, and Mehya continued to watch her grapes hang well out of reach. Lornamair's presence could only mean that the stranger was dead, and why not? What difference had anyone else been able to make? Mehya could only imagine the suffering that was in store for her because of her collusion with the newcomer. It didn't matter; her mind was already retreating to that place of grim enlightenment that elevated it above any amount of pain her captor could inflict. What could she do that hadn't already been done? Death, at this point, would be a welcome reprieve, but when had she ever been that lucky?

Lornamair moved to the well, her steps feather-light as always, and sat down on its edge. She crossed her legs in a characteristically feminine manner and looked at Mehya. Mehya didn't return the gaze, already knowing that it was blazing with hatred and threatening with violence. She merely stared at the ground, seeing nothing, waiting for the inevitable wave of the goddess's fury to once again shower her with pain and misery. Lornamair was in no hurry. What was time to an immortal? She knew that the anticipation was every bit as agonizing as the beatings themselves—that was why she never hurried. It was all a game. She did what she did because she enjoyed it.

Mehya, who was barely there to begin with, almost didn't notice when Lornamair took in a deep breath and let it out slowly. The sound wasn't hostile; something was wrong. When Mehya finally gathered enough courage to look at Lornamair, she was more than puzzled to discover that her eyes weren't hostile, either. Still, Mehya was too numb to feel anything, and when Lornamair spoke she didn't believe the words she heard.

"Your champion has convinced me to let you go," Lornamair said, her voice suggesting that she knew very well the gravity of what she was saying. *Another trick,* Mehya's dead mind responded, *and crueler than most.*"A big part of me doesn't feel good about it," Lornamair continued, "but I've decided that it's the right thing to do." Mehya's expression didn't change; her incredulity was impenetrable. "I don't feel as though I owe you an explanation, and I don't feel as though I owe you an apology," she finished. The two of them sat in silence until Lornamair stood and walked over to Mehya's rock. *Here it comes,* her mind told her.

Lornamair reached back, but her hand never came around to swing at Mehya's face. Instead it went to the string at her waist, the one that held her skirt together, and brought back a long iron key. Mehya felt nothing. Lornamair knelt down at her feet and put the key into the shackle that had for so long kept Mehya a prisoner of the island and all its damnable rocks. Mehya felt nothing. Lornamair turned the key, and there was a loud*click* and the feeling of dead weight being lifted off of her ankle—for the first time in years Mehya could feel the breeze there, where before her skin had been suffocated and damp. Still she felt nothing. Lornamair stood and looked at her squarely.

"Don't try to swim," she said, "you'll never make it. Go down to the beach and wait for me there. I'll take you home." She turned and disappeared into the forest, and Mehya could only stare after her, suddenly knowing that she was free.

Ben had absolutely no idea how much time had passed, but he didn't care. Sleeping felt just as good now as it ever did. This particular sleep was special, though. With this sleep would come an answer; he knew because of who was in his dream with him. It was Lornamair—the only person he had known in a long time who wasn't interested in keeping secrets. She would help him figure it out. She might even know the answer already; maybe all he had to do was ask. No, that would be the case if it was actually Lornamair in front of him. But he was dreaming. She wouldn't know anything that his subconscious didn't know. He could tell, because there was something different about her tonight.

He was sitting where he had when they first met, only this time he wasn't worn out from plowing through her island's jungle. He wasn't covered in sweat and blood, and his muscles weren't screaming from strain. Everything was calm. The forest was a gentle, blackish-green hue that Lornamair's skin absorbed as she looked down on him. She stood exactly as he remembered—like an empress, only now she was more dressed for the part. She was wearing an emerald green evening gown that sparkled with light from an unknown source. It split at her hips, revealing the taught, shapely leg that she had pushed forward when she first spoke to him. She was wearing shiny, green leather shoes with four-inch heels that laced all the way up her calves to just below her knees, and Ben noted how much taller they made her appear. Her neckline highlighted what was already impossible for any man to ignore, and her shoulders and back were bare except for two slim straps that held the contraption up. Odd, that she would be seen like this. Did her attire mean something, or was this simply how his subconscious wanted to see her? There was no denying that the girl, despite her murderous demeanor, was actually quite stunning.

She spoke without moving her lips, her words accompanied only by slight facial expressions that barely found their way through the darkness. *You're a fool,* she said. *You don't know me. You don't know anything about me.* Ben just continued to stare, mesmerized by the entirety of her outfit. *So how do you know so much about me?* The question was unfair and confusing, and—

Ben woke up and the light of midday hurt his eyes. He rolled over to shield his face from the sun, and discovered that it still hurt to move. There on his mattress, he did his best to recollect his dream. What kind of a question was that? This time, the truth needed no thought process to be uncovered. It came to him quickly, and as simply as he could have added two and two. If it hadn't hurt so much to laugh, he would have done exactly that, loudly and with reckless abandon. How could he have been so careless? How could he have let one mundane detail pull the wool over his eyes for so long? It wasn't important. Now he knew, and now he needed to figure out what it meant and what to do with it.

His thoughts were interrupted by the faint sound of a woman's voice. It was coming from over the drop, down on the beach, and it sounded as though it could have been Lornamair's. Feeling that it was probably time to stretch his legs a bit anyway, Ben got up as quickly as he dared and gingerly went close enough to the drop to look down. Lornamair and Mehya were standing face to face in the sand, just beyond the reach of the breaking waves, and Lornamair had Mehya's strict attention.

"You are not forgiven," she was saying. Ben was barely able to make out the words over the waves. "Do not take for granted this second chance that you're getting. You remember what it means to love someone, and do not stray from it, or I swear to all the gods you ever worshipped, I will come for you."

Mehya, whose expression was impossible to read, nodded her understanding.

"Are you ready?" Lornamair asked. Again, Mehya nodded. Lornamair took her hand and walked her out into the ocean until the water was deep enough to cover their knees. Then she put Mehya's arms at her sides and pulled her close, wrapping her up in an embrace that was more bear hug than anything else. Ben saw the way she locked her wrists behind Mehya's back and was instantly curious about what Lornamair intended to do. Suddenly she lifted Mehya off the ground and pressed their mouths together. Mehya's feet started to kick as though she was trying to free herself, but before she could accomplish anything Lornamair tipped them both to the side and they disappeared under the water with a crash and a spraying of sea foam that seemed surreal. The water there was clear, but Ben could only see a silhouette of the two women floating just under the water's surface. Then, without warning, Lornamair kicked her legs in an intriguingly dolphin-like manner and the two of them shot off at an impossible pace away from the island. Ben watched, amazed, until moments later when their shared underwater shape was far out of sight. She must have decided to let them go.

"Incredible," he said to himself. "Absolutely incredible."

Days later, Lornamair came out of the Den and found Ben sitting upright, awake.

"It's good to see you're up," she said casually.

"How long has it been since you put me here?" Ben wanted to know.

"You've been in and out for about a week," she told him. "Do you remember any of it?"

"Not really," he admitted. "But I remember my dreams. I had one about you."

"Really?" She asked, not at all interested in the details. Ben hadn't planned on giving her any. She probably wouldn't appreciate being pictured as she had been, and he was thankful that she couldn't read minds the way she could read emotions. "You'll be happy to know I let them go," she said, sitting at the end of his mattress.

"I am happy to know that," he said, remembering what he had seen down on the beach. "Does this mean that you'll be looking for something else to live for?"

"It does...I suppose," she returned. "I've found that you were right about much of what you said. My purpose here is gone now, anyway."

"It's good to hear you say that," Ben said, "because I've had a lot of time to think..."

"Why are you nervous?" Lornamair asked, her face curious. "It feels cold in my arms and hot in my face."

"Oh... right, sorry," Ben stammered.

"It's getting worse."

"How does that work, exactly?" Ben asked, flustered. "You just... feel things that people feel?" Lornamair nodded. "Could you knock it off?"

"Could you 'knock off' being nervous?" Lornamair countered. "It doesn't feel good to me, either."

Ben took her point and got himself together. *Get it over with,* he admonished himself. "I just wanted you to know that you're welcome to come with me."

"Of course I am," Lornamair said. "This is your idea, not mine; it's only fair that you at least help me into it."

Ben, who assumed that Lornamair would have needed pause to think, found himself pausing. For some reason, presenting her with that option had felt the same as when he had asked his first date to the prom. No man expected an answer in the affirmative that quickly. Then again, the analogy wasn't a very good one. It didn't necessarily make practical sense for a girl to go to the prom with any given guy, as it did for Lornamair to stay with Ben. After all, he was officially the only human being she personally knew.

"Of course you are," Ben agreed absently, still a bit stunned. "I have to go to Luna before we leave, though," he said finally. "There's one more loose end that needs to be tied up."

"If that's what you want to do," Lornamair replied cautiously. "Are you sure you don't just want to leave?"

"This has to happen," Ben insisted. "It'll be the last thing, I promise."

She nodded, breathing deeply. "Then we'll leave at sunset. How are your legs?"

"Better," he said, drawing his knees up to his chest and stretching them back out. "Still a little sore, but nothing I can't walk on. I've been moving around a bit while you were gone."

Lornamair paused indecisively. "Lindsey told me to tell you something," she said.

"Whatever it is, I don't want to hear it," Ben said curtly. "Closure is overrated."

"Good," she said, obviously relieved. "That's what I told her. She's the only one left here—are you sure you want me to let her go?"

Ben chuckled to himself before answering. "Yeah, I'm sure," he said. "But thanks for the offer. My life won't be improved by knowingly letting someone stay tied to a log somewhere. Let her get on with her life. Lord knows I have to get on with mine."

"I envy your understanding," said Lornamair.

"I don't understand," said Ben, "I only accept." Lornamair finally took her eyes off the horizon and looked at him. "With the way that the world is now, we have to accept. Things like what happened to you and I are going to happen, but we can't let them tell us who we are. Our only choice is to get back up. When you get down to it, our lives don't belong to anyone but us, and we can't go through life blaming the choices we make on the things that we go through. We can either deal with what comes, or we can all just stay secluded on our own little island, hating the world for what we feel like it did to us and never really giving ourselves a chance to move on. That isn't what I want my life to be." Even as he finished his sentence, he knew that that was exactly what he had been allowing his life to be. He drew a breath in and let it out slowly. "I wish I had known then what I know now."

"Don't we both?" Lornamair asked rhetorically. "I'm going to take Lindsey back to the mainland; from then on she can take care of herself. You and I will go across after the sun sets. I'd rather stay hidden, with your permission."

"How is it that you speak so remarkably well?" Ben wanted to know. "If Luna and this island are the only places you've ever been?"

"I never said that," was the simple reply. "Besides, I read a lot."

Ben stared at her a moment, expecting some elaboration, which she didn't offer. "Fair enough," he said, grinning. "See you when you get back."

Reckoning

If there was one thing Ben would miss about Lornamair's island it was the way the sun painted it as it went down in the evening. He hadn't really had the chance to appreciate it on the first night he arrived, something that standing on the beach with her now made him regret. There was something about the sight that almost made it hard to remember the last week and the unwelcome revelations it had brought with it. Nature had a way of reminding Ben that there was more to life than what he had, wife or no wife. At the time it was a comfortable and welcome reminder.

They were standing in water up to Ben's knees; Lornamair was submerged a bit deeper. It was just as he had seen her and Mehya do days earlier.

"My new life starts soon," Lornamair said. "Aren't you going to wish me luck?"

"Good luck," Ben said. He was very apprehensive about what he had seen her do with Mehya, and was having trouble focusing.

"You're nervous again. Don't be," she said. "This won't be the first time I've kissed you."

She reached up and pulled Ben's face into hers, forcing his mouth open and breathing into it as though trying to resuscitate him. The next thing he felt was her surprisingly powerful embrace all but squeeze the life out of him before the disorienting feeling of falling took over. The water was warm and black under the starry sky, and it muffled the sound of Lornamair's legs kicking forcefully down into it with a tremendous splash. He felt water rushing past them, trying to pull him from Lornamair's arms, but her strength never wavered. She held him tightly, and after a few moments he realized that he was underwater and breathing—he was breathing the air that she was putting into his lungs from her own. Just before he could be completely astonished, he was asleep.

He woke up to the feeling of warped lumber against his back. Opening his eyes and blinking a few times revealed nothing but a sky full of stars that was the centerpiece of another one of Luna's signature cloudless nights. He heard the sound of small waves breaking softly on sand, this time unaccompanied by the harshness of larger ones barreling through rock formations and into natural walls. He sat up on the dock and looked around, shivering as the breeze informed him that his clothes were soaking wet again. Lornamair was sitting on the end of it just a few feet away, staring at him coolly.

"I'll wait here," she said, not sounding as though it was open for debate. "I'd rather not be seen. Just come get me when you're done."

"It'll only take a few minutes," Ben said, getting up and stretching his arms and legs before starting to walk. Roger's house was just up the hill and on the right, and when Ben reflected on the last week he thought it was the easiest seven hundred feet he had ever traveled. He walked calmly up the porch steps and knocked deliberately enough to be heard, but passively enough to not alarm whoever was inside. After almost half a minute the knob turned and Roger had the door halfway open before he froze, staring at what he thought must have been a ghost. He opened the door slowly from that point on, his eyes uncertain and his body tense.

"Ben," he said, affording him an arbitrary nod.

"Roger," Ben said, returning the gesture. "Has everyone had time to settle in?"

"A few of them are not in good shape," Roger told him. "They had been out there too long... it is good to see you."

"Really?" Ben asked, glaring. The look in his eyes told Roger that he should find some friendly ground in a hurry.

"Did you find your wife?"

"Yes, I did, thank you." Ben's face was frozen in a mask of business-like anger, and Roger, ever the diplomat, came outside and closed the door behind him, hoping that he would be able to diffuse Ben's problem before things heated up.

"Good, good," Roger said, trying to decide where to take the conversation. Ben saved him the trouble.

"Of course," he continued, "my reunion with my wife wasn't the happiest. I was disappointed to learn what she had been up to, as you might've suspected. I imagine news like that isn't easy for anyone to take, though. How did *your* wife take it when *she* found out?"

"...I'm sorry?" Roger said, seeing for the first time that Ben knew much more than he was supposed to.

"You know her name," Ben said softly. "If no one here has ever seen her and lived to tell about it, how do you know her name?" Roger continued to stare at him. "When I got to that island," Ben explained, "when I first met her, I asked her how she knew my name, and she told me that she had obviously been spending time with someone who knew me; I never thought to ask myself how I already had a name for her. I heard it from you." He thought it was refreshing that Roger didn't bother to try and cover anything else up.

"Ben, it was just business," he said. "As a businessman yourself, I'm sure you can understand."

"Of course I do," Ben said, feeling himself getting angrier by the second. "I understand that you knew that I would probably die out there, and you also knew that if I didn't then I would come back knowing things that you don't want anyone knowing because if the people here were aware of her reasons she might attract some sympathy. I understand that you wanted me to kill someone who has already gone through god knows how many lifetimes of suffering because she was standing in the way of industrial progress. I understand that somehow you convinced the only friend I thought I had to leave me stranded out there to die in case I succeeded and that you would've carried on with business as usual once it was all swept under the rug. You may not have enough money to develop anything, but you have enough to bribe, don't you? You must have gotten a hold of Chris before we ever came out here. I'm curious to know how much it took."

"It did not take any," Roger said, his voice quiet and defensive. "He knew he could not stop you from coming and he did not want to have to face you in case you lived and found out what had happened. If I had not told him to leave you out there he probably would have anyway."

"Well it's good to know we're all holding ourselves accountable," Ben said with dark sarcasm. "I wouldn't want you to lose any sleep while you cash in on your empire."

Now it was Roger's turn to get angry. "Do not think you know so much!" He spat harshly. "The people in Luna have had to live in poverty because of her grudges! As long as she took it upon herself to nab husbands and wives this place would never improve! Think about what happened to you—we would have been partners if she had not interfered. She was never willing to let Luna move on and the world is a better place without her!"

Ben let his volume rise to match Roger's. "It was all she knew to do. How long have you been sending people out there to kill her?" He asked. "Since the first, probably. Someone had to start sending people in that direction and as near as I can tell that someone could only be the person who drove her out there to begin with. *You're* the reason she was out there, *you're* the reason she was angry, and you've been sending other people out there to clear your own conscience while you stayed here and hid behind good intentions. *She was never able to move on because you never let her!*"

"No one forced her to kidnap innocent people in retaliation for what she thinks I did to her," Roger said. "What was I to do? Her mind was set. Her hatred was complete. You must have found out for yourself that there is no changing that woman. I could not stand by and let her terrorize my people, whatever her reasons." He read the look on Ben's face perfectly, and his eyes softened after a moment; he understood where the mixture of cynicism and contempt was coming from, knew why the traces of a wry smile found their way into his otherwise angry countenance. "You think I sound like a hypocrite," Roger stated.

Ben's voice was even. "I have to wonder what kind of man, or god for that matter, wouldn't handle a problem like this himself."

"She would have killed me," Roger said, "and my work is too important to be sacrificed for the sake of my honor. It may sound weak to you, but I believe in what I do. You do not understand the spell that the idea of love has held over these people. It takes their will to live, Ben. It means everything, and it takes everything."

"I might understand better than you think," Ben said. "But if she had wanted you dead, you would be. She came and went to and from this town as she pleased—what stopped her from ending your life, if that's what she wanted?"

"She did not realize I was still here," Roger answered.

Ben had to think about what he had just heard. "How is that possible?"

"She was never interested in what had become of me after she left," Roger explained. "She went off to nurse her wounds and I am sure that she assumed that I fled Luna, but I stayed."

"And she never saw you?" Ben pressed. "She never *felt* you?"

"Yes, she was acutely sensitive to feelings, was she not? She could feel disturbances in people when things were not as they usually were. It was her gift. When I first thought of joining this society, when my curiosity first piqued, she knew. My decision to leave enraged her, but after that, what was there for her to sense? I feel the same way now as I did the day I left her; there has been no disturbance in me."

Despite knowing Lornamair no longer than a week, Ben knew her better than anyone else on Earth, and he also knew that Roger was making sense. He doubted that Lornamair bothered to take in the sights when she came to Luna on her kidnapping missions, so as long as her target wasn't sleeping in Roger's house she would have never had a reason to explore it and find him there. And she never felt him because— no, not *never* felt him—*always* felt him. The pain of his actions had stayed with her, and now Ben thought he knew why she could never let it go—because it had never actually left, unbeknownst even to her. She assumed that the problem was internal, being mostly unable to differentiate between what she felt on her own and the feelings that she absorbed from others. As it turned out, she had simply been wrong. The source of her agony had been there in Luna all along.

Ben's head spun as he tried to get a grip on what it all meant. Roger studied Ben's frown and took a guess as to its cause. "This is difficult to believe, yes?" He asked.

"Actually, no," Ben replied. "It's just very unfortunate how off base you are about the dramatically dependent relationship you think your people have with love." Roger seemed mildly amused at the thought of some foreigner knowing his people better than he did, but didn't interrupt as Ben made his point. "There's something that the people here don't know about Lornamair's victims...she only took the unfaithful."

For a moment, the strange expression on Roger's face didn't change. Then it dissolved into a smile and he looked at the floor sheepishly, laughing to himself.

"Is something funny?" Ben wanted to know, positive that he wasn't going to appreciate the joke.

"Tell me," Roger said, "did you encounter any men out there on her island?"

There it was again. That panicky feeling that told him that he needed to be looking in all directions at once because he was about to be blindsided by reality once again clamped onto his heart and squeezed. He wasn't surprised that Roger knew there were no men out there; after all, he had been present for all of the disappearances. What worried him was that he didn't see immediately why the question was relevant. Ben thought that Roger's question had been rhetorical, but when Roger didn't continue, he answered curtly.

"No, I didn't," Ben said, struggling to find patience.

"Surely you must have thought that very strange," Roger said. "It takes more than one person to be unfaithful."

"Of course I thought it was strange," Ben said, exasperated and wondering why answers had to be so damned slow coming. "But I had bigger problems at the time than worrying about her clientele. I figured she never took any because they were from out of town, maybe, and didn't stay long enough to get nabbed just by coincidence. It's shaky, I know, but it was the best I could do. It's *still* the best I can do; I can't think of any other reason why she never felt—"

"Not never," Roger interrupted. *"Always."*

Ben blinked—twice—before his mind had time to react. If the last week had been any less incredible than it had been, Roger's statement might have floored him. As it was, revelations like these were becoming par for the course. Feeling like some oblivious idiot was becoming second nature.

"You're kidding me," was just about all he could get out.

"Certainly not," Roger insisted. "It would be fair to say that the women she took ended up on her island because of me."

It was no wonder that Ben had been unable to figure so much of this business out for himself. Every answer he got led to more and more questions. "And how did you pull that off so many times, may I ask?" Ben's curiosity was getting the better of him. To him, this phenomenon was one of the most mystifying parts of the entire drama. "I don't mean any offense, but you don't look like anything special. If the people here are so taken with the idea of love, how could you or anyone else convince them to leave it behind, even for a few hours?"

Roger's smile was knowing and genuine when he spoke. "Remember, I was worshipped as a god here once, and I have my ways," he said cryptically. "These people are quite taken with love, as you say, but do they really understand the nature of it? I think not. They are human, and they have impulses. I am merely the only one here who had cause to exploit them."

"Fair enough," said Ben, not entirely satisfied with the answer, not entirely surprised that he wasn't. "So what was this cause? Your concern for the wellbeing of the people here seems genuine enough, so why play with their emotions like you have? Why create rifts between people who love each other?"

"I had hoped to show them that love is not everything," Roger said solemnly. "But things such as those cannot simply be told. And even if they could, who among the people here would believe me? No, my observance of your kind, along with my own history, has assured me that the only reliable learning is done through experience. At first, that was my motivation. I could see the spiral that love can cause—saw it in my own companion. Possessiveness, jealousy, the fear of loss—if I had let it continue, Luna would have ended up...well, exactly where it has ended up." Roger looked distant, thoughtful, and full of regret. "It was not until much later that I felt I had to get rid of her for the sake of Luna's future." Ben was no longer digging for information, but Roger continued, lost in memories as the flood of admissions and honesty kept his words coming. "It was not an easy decision," he said, shaking his head sadly. "Do you think I *wanted* to see her killed? If there had been any other way...but she does not allow for other ways." Hints of anger found their way back into Roger's voice. "If she had only *attempted* to understand...so many things I wanted to show these people. Their idea of an infallible, yet very fragile bond of love had to be uprooted if they were to progress as a society. The knowledge that there are greater causes than our own indulgences and ideas of what we want for ourselves—*that* is what I wanted to impart to my people." Roger's eyes found Ben's, and suddenly he was back in the present. "And now look at us," he said, his voice just short of a growl. "The people of Luna have gotten nowhere."

"The plan looked good on paper, right?" Ben said, hoping that Roger would get the analogy.

Roger's face softened again, and he let out a short, resigned laugh. "I suppose it did, indeed," he said. "So close, yet so far away from success."

"And you think that Lornamair was entirely responsible for its failure?"

"It is impossible to know whether or not the experiences these women had with me were enough to shake them out of love's hypnotic hold on their hearts and minds," Roger admitted. "If I had been given the opportunity to see the results of my experiment, I could have tried a different approach upon seeing it fail. But it was the best idea I had. I still feel that the theory was sound, but—"

"But I never gave them the chance to reflect on, or share, the experience with anyone else, so whatever learning they did never caught on."

The voice had come from around the corner of the house at Roger's back, and its arrival startled both men. They both knew instantly who it belonged to, but Ben was much quicker to recover from the little shock than Roger was. Not that anyone would have been able to tell. Ben would've expected Roger to wheel around, or at least blink, or maybe even bolt off the porch and head, as fast as he could, in whatever direction would take him farthest from the source of that voice. Of course, no one would have known better than Roger how futile running away would be. Instead, he didn't move. He didn't blink. He continued to look at Ben, although it was obvious that he was no longer actually seeing him. His facial expression didn't change, his body didn't tense, his eyes didn't water. He showed no sign of being startled, much less afraid, yet somehow it was precisely that reaction which told Ben that he was terrified—evidently, terrified beyond the range of verbal or physical expression.

Ben couldn't blame him; Lornamair's arrival had a way of making people lose control of their faculties.

He could only imagine what the moment must have been like for Roger, who had made the mistake of assuming that Ben's survival and return to Luna meant Lornamair's death. All those years of going undetected, and now that single miscalculation might very well cost him everything.

For a few breaths, Roger was frozen. In the next, he was resigned. He slowly turned around as Lornamair rounded the corner of the house, stepping out of the shadows and into the soft light emanating from the lamp that was mounted over Roger's front door.

"I probably should have mentioned that neither of us felt that the other had to die," Ben said, getting entirely too much satisfaction out of the fact that he finally had a surprise of his own to spring on someone else for a change. Roger didn't respond as his eyes met with his wife's; the moment was simply too sublime to acknowledge the obvious or appreciate the humor in sarcasm.

Lornamair's expression was completely unreadable. "It's been a long time, my love," she said quietly.

Roger barely nodded. "Yes, it has."

Lornamair cocked her head a bit and eyed him dryly. *"Roger,"* she said disdainfully. "What a foolish name. Your given name was much more beautiful."

"Beauty is in the eye of the beholder, my queen." To Roger's credit, he now seemed largely un-rattled, either resigned to his presumed fate or showing flashes of hidden majesty. "I will not apologize for this name or any other."

To Ben, Roger's transformation was incredible. Once a smooth-talking, amiable, endearingly odd-mannered diplomat, he was now resolute, noble, and going toe to toe with the most terrifying creature Ben had ever had the opportunity to meet. Maybe, he thought, he was about to find out what it was like to see two gods battle.

"And certainly not for the hearts you broke," Lornamair said accusingly. A spiteful smile touched the corners of her mouth. "Those little harlots didn't even know it was you, did they?"

"Of course not," Roger said evenly. "And you should be careful with your accusations. No hearts were broken until you decided to take the fate of these people into your own hands."

"Even so, why not show them who you are? Why all the lies?" Lornamair wanted to know.

Roger's response was sure and without hesitation. "Revealing my identity would have had unforeseeable consequences on the community due to my status here," he said. "Besides, the last thing the people of Luna need is another god to fear."

Lornamair visibly recoiled at that, but came back at her husband that much harder. "The only thing you ever wanted for this 'community' was to turn it into a brothel and call it heaven," she declared. "Tell me, what is the difference between enslaving people with chains and enslaving them with impulse?"

"My intention," Roger growled, "was to point out that there *is* none. Enslavement is the same whether through chains, impulse, love, or any other means of manipulation. And do not pretend to care about the wellbeing of these people. Falseness does not become you."

Lornamair glared. "They never learned anything, you know. Mostly they just felt sorry for themselves. You accomplished nothing."

Roger didn't miss a beat. "If they learned nothing during their stay with you, then I was not alone in my lack of progress. All the more reason, I would think, to abandon your idiotic crusade."

It was no secret that Lornamair was getting fired up. Her hands had curled into fists, and her glare was as intense as Ben had ever seen it. Again, Roger deserved credit for standing his ground, knowing full well that Lornamair had been waiting for centuries to rip his heart out of his chest and use it as her own personal hacky sack. "Still as unapologetic as ever," she pointed out.

"Naturally, that is why you are here," Roger said. "Not to see an end to this ridiculous feud, not to simply declare an end to your reign of terror over the people here, not even to check on the wellbeing of your new friend here, but because of some selfish idea that you are owed something. You have come here looking for some sign of my remorse and have been disappointed. So I wonder—what will you decide to take from me now that you have me again? You want an apology for the way things have turned out? Well, that you have. I am truly sorry for what has happened between us. I regret, every day, that we were never able to reconcile, and that the people of Luna have had to suffer so much because of it. I regret, every day, the way that my departure has made you feel. But again, *I believe in what I am doing*. I believe in a purpose greater than my own sense of satisfaction, and I regret that you were never able to understand that. It was never my intention to hurt you, and I regret that that has been the result of what I have done."

Lornamair's jaw was set, and her eyes had welled up with tears, reminding Ben again of how fragile her tough, unforgiving exterior was. When she spoke at last, her voice was a whimper.

"I've had to feel it all," she cried. *"I've had to feel the pain that sets in when love is lost, and the insanity that follows after. I have lived the cycle every day, and never, never have you shown me mercy. Never have you let me rest."* She winced and lowered her head, as if feeling some indescribable pain that was sharp and deep in her core. Roger opened his mouth to respond, but before he could Lornamair dashed forward with supernatural speed and jacked him up against his front door. Ben noticed that Roger had actually tried to defend himself, but whatever he was, he was not as physically strong or as fast as his wife. Her eyes shone malevolence in the soft porch light, and she shoved her words through her teeth as she admonished him, pinning both of his shoulders against the door with her hands. ***"Tell me you owe me nothing!"*** She ordered, the madness electrifying the deep green hue of her irises. ***"Tell me how selfish I am! Tell me how vindictive! Tell me I need to grow up!"*** She stopped shaking Roger and pulled herself close, so that he was forced to look almost straight down to maintain the eye contact that he knew she demanded. ***"Tell me why I shouldn't tear your arms out of their sockets and beat you to death with them. Show me your face, and tell me."***

Her last sentence struck Ben as strange until Roger, who had no options whatsoever, began to age in reverse right before his eyes. Ben watched in silent disbelief as Roger's height increased by two or three inches, and the faint lines in his face disappeared. His hair grew out to shoulder length, and the muscles in his arms became more defined. In a matter of seconds, he had gone from soft and middle-aged to—well, to godly.

Lornamair seemed to get some satisfaction out of his compliance, but didn't let up on the pressure she was applying. Roger gathered himself and spoke again.

"I have no doubt that your gift is intended to serve a purpose," he told her. "And I am sorry for the burden it has been."

"How can you say that when you have no idea what a burden it's been?" She asked him, calmer, but still very volatile. "You're apologizing for everything you can't control. What about the rest? *What about the decision **you made** to abandon me?*"

"I have already said that I did not feel as though I had a choice," Roger insisted. "I have already said that I am sorry for what happened," he said, mildly bewildered.

"That isn't the same thing," Ben said. "She understands that you did what you felt like you had to do. What she doesn't understand is why you won't accept what comes with it. It's true that she made her own decisions. But she could just as easily use the same logic in reverse."

"And I have," Lornamair said. "Until Ben showed up, I was convinced that all of this was your fault, just as you are that it's mine. But I have accepted responsibility for my part in all of it." She took her hands off of Roger and backed away a step, looking at him earnestly while he shifted uncomfortably, doubtlessly uncertain of what she was going to do.

Ben knew very well the struggle that was taking place in the innermost part of his new friend's psyche. She appeared to be collecting herself, but that was almost definitely not the case. There were dark places inside that soul. There were centuries of hatred and contempt, lifetimes of hurt and cruelty, that were not simply going to go away in a week. Lornamair had come a long way, but her journey toward letting go was far—very far—from over. Every fiber of her being was screaming for the one thing that had made her life worth living—vengeance. Every promise she had made to herself about accountability, every oath she had sworn in the name of retribution, vindication, and justice was lunging its way to the forefront of her mind, demanding satisfaction, insisting that she rip this self-righteous fool limb from limb. Here it was. The moment she had been waiting for. The encounter that she had so longed for in isolation across the sea, the chance to make good on every grisly threat she had silently screamed from her prison in the midst of the ocean, the opportunity to unleash her fury on its own source—here it was. The primal urge to tear him apart was overwhelming. She should beat him until he recognized the error of his ways, and then she should keep beating him until there was nothing left to beat. She should make him endure hundreds of years of pain, and then tell him that he only had himself to thank for it. She should drag him around and use his face to shatter all the remnants of his pathetic human life to pieces, so that he would see how temporary it all was—the glass in his windows, the lamps, the furniture—and exactly how dire a mistake his decision to leave her alone had been.

Her thoughts grew darker still…

Maybe she should just take back what was hers. Maybe she should go home, and take her husband with her. There were plenty of ways to ensure that he would never leave her again. He would object, but what would it matter? What problems could possibly arise when there would be no one to hear him scream? She should have done that in the beginning, then this whole mess never would have come about. They could live together forever, and things would be just as they were intended to be from the start. He would love her again, given enough time. And what was time to an immortal? Why should she care about what he wanted?

This moment, this agonizingly eternal moment, had been generations in the making. Ben had done his best to impress upon Lornamair the importance of letting go, but now that her moment had arrived, she would do as she pleased. He could only stand by and hope that she found it somewhere within herself to do the right thing. His heart sank when he saw the dreamy expression that made its way over her face as she kept staring at Roger, knowing that her mind was somewhere else entirely and not liking at all where it seemed it had chosen to go. Roger noticed and closed his eyes, preparing for the absolute worst.

No, not like this, he told himself. *It's been too much work, and there's too much to lose. Snap her out of it.* Unfortunately, he had no idea how to snap her out of it. *Say something.*

"Please," he said meekly. Lornamair's head involuntarily jerked toward him just a tick. "Not like this," he pleaded quietly. "Please."

Lornamair shook her head briskly, and the clarity returned to her eyes. She turned toward Ben and gave him a knowing look, like a dog who had been caught chewing shoes—a little ashamed, and desperate for some understanding. Maybe even wanting permission to keep on chewing...

Ben shook his head slowly, praying that she got his point, and left the rest to fate. Her eyes fell a moment in reflection, and then she turned and looked again at Roger. What the moment of truth offered were words that, just days ago, he never expected would have escaped her lips.

"I'm sorry for making your life so difficult. Please forgive me."

Once the words were out, Lornamair was more than a little surprised to discover that they felt right. It didn't seem fair, but they felt *right*. While she was trying to figure out how fair and right could occupy two places at once, she didn't notice Roger's reaction until he spoke.

"I also apologize for what I have done to you," he said. "I hope you can forgive me, as I will forgive you."

And then, in one of history's most profound and astounding moments, the reasons ceased to matter, if only temporarily. The sheer impossibility of it all made what was happening seem unreal. Gone was the vengeance, gone were the lies, burned away by the liberating feeling of genuine, basic love. For a few seconds, they felt it again—a glimpse of a past that both of them dearly missed, of a time when they were uninterrupted and ignorant of the rest of the world and its infinite follies. They both comprehended something truly incredible then—that with that one friendly gesture, which had been the first between them since the dawn of their existences, they became something so much more meaningful and rewarding than lovers. In that instant, they were friends.

Lornamair, who processed emotions to an exponential degree to begin with, barely had any idea at all how she should react. This man had once been her eternal lover, and later, her mortal enemy, but never her friend. She looked at Ben, who was still standing by and staying out of the way, with teary eyes, stunned and asking for advice. Ben didn't want to sully the moment by speaking, but he gave her an impatient glance and subtly jerked his head in Roger's direction as if to say, *well, go ahead.*

Lornamair looked back at Roger, then quickly down at her feet, then back up at Roger. Too much water had collected in her eyes at that point, and the tears flowed freely when she spoke. "Of course I do," she whispered. Then she smiled and her eyes were pleading as she repeated, "Of course I do."

Roger, undoubtedly paralyzed by seeing his wife forgive someone (particularly *him*), made no move as the flood of new emotions made Lornamair weak in the knees. Ben saw what was happening and darted forward as she fell out, catching her just before the collapse was complete. Roger remained in a daze while Ben scooped her up and carried her over to the bench that had faithfully remained the only piece of furniture on the porch over the years. He sat her upright at one end of it and sat down next to her, leaning her head against his shoulder.

After a minute he asked Roger, who hadn't yet moved from where he had been pinned against his front door, "Are you all right?"

Roger blinked and looked at Ben as if he had just seen one of Luna's fish jump out of the ocean and do the Charleston all the way up the stretch. "She forgave me," he said.

"I had a feeling she might," Ben said. "She's not quite what I was told she was." He gave his jab a moment to sink in before he continued. "Neither are you." Roger said nothing. "It's quite a talent you have there, the aging thing," Ben continued. "I don't suppose you could explain it?"

"I am afraid not," Roger answered. "It is how I was made."

Lornamair lifted her head off of Ben's shoulder and sat up slowly, steadying herself. "He appears however he chooses," she said. "It's his gift, and certainly the reason that the people here don't realize what he is."

"My gift was my compassion, queen," Roger said pointedly. "This business with appearances is, as Ben said, only talent. And yes, it is how I keep my secret. I appear to age normally, and when I am old, I stage my death. Within a few weeks, I reinsert myself into this society as a baby and begin the cycle again—new name, new body."

And at last, it all made sense. As much sense as it could make.

Roger walked over and sat down on the bench next to Ben, searching for words. It was several minutes before he found them. "Ben," he said, "I realize what has happened here. I realize what I have done. I know that I have lied to you, I have put you in danger, and I have given you more than one reason to hate me. Still, here we sit, and I owe you a debt of gratitude that I will never be able to repay. You brought closure to a situation that I thought was beyond all hope, and you did it without bringing harm to anyone, which is more than I can say for my own efforts. It appears that I should have had much more faith in you than I did. I have been reunited with my wife, and we can finally let the past be the past. All of this is because of your courage and heart, and it will never be forgotten."

"I understand why things happened the way they did," Ben said. "There are no hard feelings."

"You are a better friend than I deserve," said Roger. "I never would have imagined anyone could convince her to let it go. How were you so sure that bringing her here would not end in disaster?"

Ben shook his head. "I told her to stay behind," he said. "I didn't know she was going to follow me. I came here for another reason entirely."

It was hard for Ben to decipher expressions on Roger's newly formed, younger-looking face, but he guessed that at the moment it was showing something between apprehension and mild surprise. Roger took a long look past Ben at Lornamair, who simply looked back at him, and then asked, "What reason?"

Ben found Roger's apprehension amusing. It was obvious that the only people who weren't terrified of his new friend were the ones who didn't know her. It seemed so strange now that she was sitting next to him, minding her own business. When she wasn't shooting daggers with her eyes (or threatening someone's life) one could almost say she looked downright docile. Simply incredible, it was, how close to the surface her innate hostility stayed.

"Well," Ben said, "it seems to me that most of this is behind us now, and I haven't forgotten how it all started. So," he said, taking a breath, "I came here to tell you that you and I can move forward with our venture, if your interest is still there."

It took Roger a palpable second or two to get up to speed, and when he did, he only blinked. Interestingly, the only sign of any reaction at all from him at first was the sigh that Lornamair let out beside him. He turned to look at her and saw a dreamy expression which, on anyone else's face, might not have looked as strange and alien as it did. Still, Ben was happy to see it; it was about time someone gave her something good to feel.

His attention snapped back to Roger when he finally spoke. "Ben," he said, "I could not... I have done so much..."

"I told you, I get it," Ben said, cutting short the unnecessary apology. "You have a vision, and I respect that. You've been working for what you believe is a greater good, and I respect that, too, even if I don't agree with your methods." Ben smiled softly as Roger started to shake his head. "I'm saving you the trouble of finding another financier," he said. "Don't be an idiot. You're not going to find anyone who knows Luna as well as I do."

Roger's face had been suggesting that he had been both touched and ashamed by the offer, but by the time Ben had finished speaking, he was beaming. He took Ben's hand and shook it vigorously. "Your kindness—"

He was immediately shushed by Lornamair as she looked down the stretch at the sleeping village. "We don't want Luna to wake up," she admonished. "Calm yourself."

Roger continued in a deliberate whisper, but actually calming himself was evidently a bit much to ask. He resumed shaking the hand that he hadn't let go of. "Your kindness will not be forgotten, I swear it," he told Ben as jubilantly as a whisper would allow. "When can we begin, do you suppose?"

"As soon as you're ready," Ben stated plainly. "I've seen enough. My number and my address are still the same."

"You are going home, then?" Roger asked, a trace of disappointment dampening his festive disposition.

"Oh, yes," Ben said, nodding and looking at Roger as though he had just asked if he needed air to breathe. "I've had enough vacation." He followed Lornamair's gaze down the stretch. "Come to think of it, it's probably about time we were going."

"And what will *you* do?" Roger asked Lornamair. "I could find a place for you in the village, I am sure—"

"I'm going with Ben," she said.

Roger nodded as though that was the only decision that made sense. "I am glad to hear it. Perhaps I will see you again?"

"Maybe one day, when I decide that I need a vacation," she said, grinning enigmatically. Then, after a pause, she said, "Well, until next time, then." She and Ben walked down the porch steps and out onto the stretch, all her emotions, true to form, gone for the moment.

"There is not another plane arriving here for weeks," Roger told them. "If you like, I can have a taxi come from the city. It will take time to get here, but I have no car of my own to offer you—I will see to it that your fare is taken care of for you."

"That would be fine, thank you," Ben said. "About how long 'till its arrival?"

"It is about ninety minutes' drive."

"Good enough. I'll be in touch. And thanks." They started up the stretch together toward the final stop.

"Take care of her, my friend," Roger called.

Ben turned and saw that Roger the Local God was gone, replaced once again by the amiable, odd-mannered entrepreneur he had always known—or *thought* he had always known. "I'll be surprised if

I need to," he called back, "but I get your point and I'll do my best."

"You should work on your English," Lornamair told him. "You spend more time around these people than I do, and I sound better."

Roger laughed heartily. "I never had the aptitude for it that you did," he replied. Then he added, with a shrug, "It is part of my charm!"

Roger watched the two of them walk up the stretch until the darkness of night hid them completely. Then he turned, went back inside, and continued letting the people of Luna assume that he was sleeping.

The night was a quiet one, and the only sound being made as the two travelers walked up the stretch was that of their own muffled footsteps on the soft dirt. No one had been woken during their talk with Roger, which was a blessing. It may have been true that no one would have recognized Lornamair, but Ben knew that his mission was not likely a secret in a town as small as this one. It would be no surprise if some of them were able to put two and two together, and there was no telling what might ensue once that happened.

"I'm proud of you," Ben said. "It could have gone very differently back there. How are you holding up?"

"I'm embarrassed that I didn't figure it out on my own," she told him. "Other than that, I'm really not sure how I feel."

Ben was hoping to hear something much more relieving from her, but that might have been unrealistic. Centuries of pain didn't just go away with a conversation. Now that they were out of the moment, she was free again to stew over what those centuries had been like. And she probably would. But then again, who wouldn't? Healing didn't take a course from point A to point B. It was a cycle—positive and negative emotions came and went like the tide. Sometimes it was comforting to think about the acceptance of the past, and sometimes it was impossible to remember why the past was ever accepted at all. Emotions could be complicated. Ben could only imagine what it was like to feel the emotions of others as well. Keeping that in mind, he was doing his best to stay relaxed and appreciative of the closure they had just gotten. He didn't want her honing in on any stray regrets.

When they reached the door of Micah's hut, Ben paused. "Are you sure you want to come in here?" Ben asked.

Lornamair nodded curtly. "I owe it to him."

"Stand over here to the side," Ben said. "I don't want your arrival to be abrupt. Make your presence known when you get your cue." Lornamair's brow furrowed, but she did as he asked.

Ben took a breath and knocked, praying that Micah was a light sleeper and that no one else in the immediate area was. After a moment, when there was no sign of movement from inside, he knocked again, a bit harder. Before long there was the faint sound of sheets rustling, and then a surprisingly alert Micah swung the door open. He was frowning, as anyone would have been, but lit up when he recognized the man who had called on him so late.

Ben immediately held up his hands. "I need you to keep your voice down, okay?" He asked quietly.

Micah complied effortlessly. "Yes, of course," he said. "Please, please, come in, come in." He went to his table and lit a single short candle, giving the hut a very eerie glow.

"Is it all right if I enter with a friend?" Ben asked him.

Micah straightened and looked Ben over in the dim light—not in an unfriendly manner, but in one that reflected both surprise and cautious curiosity. "Of course," he said. Ben reached over, took Lornamair's arm, and gently led her into the hut ahead of him. Ben noticed how the lighting made her haunting beauty seem even more haunting and beautiful. Micah smiled like a proud father meeting his son's prom date, and Ben knew instantly that he had no idea who had just entered his home. Like Ben, Micah had probably envisioned Lornamair as something just short of a monster; her flawless skin, healthy hair, and shapeliness were not things that he associated with the thought of her. "This one is so young, yet I do not recognize her," he said. "Did the old witch actually have prisoners from other places?"

Ben opened his mouth to respond, but he was cut short by a worried sounding voice coming from what had to be the bedroom. It was female, and elderly-sounding. "Who is it?" The voice asked tentatively.

"It is our friend, Ben," Micah told her jovially. "He has brought with him one of your fellow prisoners."

"Actually—" Ben started to say, but there was again the sound of rustling sheets. It had all the making of a head-on collision, but all he could do was stand there and listen to the soft footsteps approach the main room, picturing how badly it was all about to go. He looked nervously at Lornamair, who was watching the doorway of the bedroom steadily, doubtlessly having already accepted the inevitable.

When the old woman entered the room, there was a welcoming smile on her face that lasted about a second. She had barely even locked eyes with her former captor when she clasped her hand over her mouth in horror and pointed, wide-eyed and frantic. Instinct was first to react, and it pushed her backwards into the wall of the hut where her tears immediately started to flow, her head immediately started to shake furiously, and she broke into a fear-inspired blend of sobbing and screaming that was thankfully muffled by her hand. She slid down to the floor and continued to point, her feet scrambling on the floor in an effort to push her through the wall and as far away from Lornamair as possible. Truth be told, it was the same thing he had expected out of Roger. Micah, startled and bewildered, hurried over to her and tried futilely to calm his wife down, but she seemed unable to acknowledge him. He was in the midst of stammering an apology to his guests when he noticed what his wife was staring and pointing at, and comprehension slowly found its way into his eyes. He stood and turned, his face solemn as he saw Lornamair for who she was.

"I'm not here for you," Lornamair told his wife, her voice comforting despite doing all but licking her lips with the delicious aftertaste of horror. The statement did a world of good; the panic stopped and things quieted down, though the old woman refused to move from her seat on the floor.

Lornamair barely spared her another glance before addressing Micah. "Has she told you why she's been gone?" She asked him. Micah nodded, and then, in a curious display of indigenous superstition, he dropped to his knees and bowed his head. "Please get up," Lornamair said gently. "I'm not your god anymore." Micah looked up at her before finally standing again. "The punishment was not meant for you," she said. "I'm sorry if there was any confusion."

"Thank you for bringing her back to me," Micah said in a hoarse whisper.

"Thank *him,*" she said, looking at Ben without smiling.

Micah looked at Ben sincerely. "I thank you," he said. "Our reunion has been very emotional."

"I know," Lornamair interjected. "I hope neither of you forgets how it feels."

Ben unfastened the knives that still hung at his hips and handed them over. "I came here to give you these," he said kindly. "I want you to know that they saved my life more than once. So call us even, if you like."

"And *I* want you to know that you can both rest easy from now on," Lornamair added. "Your wife has paid her price, and I'm leaving with Ben."

Micah smiled approvingly. "You are finally going home," he said.

"That's right," Ben said. "But you'll see me around. I'm helping Roger out with his development—I hope that's all right with you."

"I have no reason to complain," Micah answered. "You go and help the world move on."

"Thank you again," Ben said. "We should let you get back to sleep. We don't want to be late for our ride. It was good to see you again—take care of her."

"Of course I will, and likewise," said Micah.

Ben turned to leave, and Lornamair, her eyes as cruel and threatening as ever, blew a kiss to the old woman in the corner. "Be good," she whispered. And out the door they went.

Immersion

Ben thought that the walk back to Roger's porch was lighthearted, all things considered. "Do you really just never want that woman to sleep again?" He asked Lornamair. "I thought you said that she paid her price. Why did you scare her, wasn't she scared enough?"

"I regret that I can't see all my beauties again before I leave," she purred. "I'd like to make sure that they remember me."

"I really doubt that that's necessary," Ben said. "They're probably *all* huddled in a corner somewhere right now, trying to figure out how to start repairing a lifetime's worth of psychological damage. Did you see what your mere presence did to that poor woman?"

"Mmm hmm," Lornamair answered, obviously proud of herself. "You may have convinced me to let them go, but I still believe that they deserved everything that they got. They're getting off light, thanks to you."

"You can't seriously think—"

"You convinced me to let them go and that should really be good enough," Lornamair said, her tone final and irritated.

"Are you really going to come back and check in on them?" Ben wanted to know, recalling what she had said to Mehya on the beach.

"No," she answered, "but they don't have to know that, do they?"

They got back to Roger's porch with some time to spare. There was no sign of him, but they both knew that he was awake. What needed to be said had been said, however, and there was probably no point in extending the goodbye.

"It feels strange to leave," Lornamair said, looking out at the night and listening to the distant lapping of water. "It feels strange to change all this."

"I think everyone will be better for it," Ben assured her.

"They already are," she said, somewhat absently. "I've made everyone so happy. It feels strange to not feel any pain, or fear, or...any of it. Everyone just feels so happy... and it feels so strange."

"Do you like it?"

"I'm not sure," she admitted, a hint of a smile turning her mouth upward. "Fear is delicious."

"How do *you* feel?"

"Tired," she said. "Like you feel at the end of a very, very long day."

"Well, it certainly has been one of those," Ben told her. Distant headlights appeared in the darkness down the main road leading into Luna. "That's us. Are you ready?" Lornamair simply nodded. They walked down the steps and went to the side of the road, waiting for the taxi. It pulled up and came to a stop at the edge of the road, where the last trace of modern civilization ended and Luna began. Crossing that threshold and stepping into the car was like taking the first official step back into a normal life for Ben, and an entirely new one for Lornamair.

The two of them settled into the back seat, and Ben made eye contact with the driver through the rear-view mirror. "Thanks for coming out all this way," Ben said to him. "This was pretty much our only option. I know you'll miss out on a few tips because of this."

The driver's voice was casual and unexpressive. "Don't worry about it, eh?" He was a big fellow, but sounded young with a slight Hispanic accent. In the meager light that the dashboard provided, Ben could see that tattoos covered his forearms and disappeared under the sleeves of his shirt. Ben watched as he adjusted the mirror to get a look at Lornamair. "As long as you can pay for the ride."

Ben sat up a little straighter. "I, uh, was told that the fare would already be taken care of." The driver readjusted his mirror, turned his palms face-up and delivered a look that said *well, nobody told* me *about it.* "I just don't have anything on me," Ben continued. "If you're patient, I can fix you up when we get to the airport."

"Sorry," the driver said, shaking his head, "don't have that kinda time, and I heard that one a buncha times already, anyway, right?" Ben sat back in his seat and looked flatly at Lornamair. Unbelievable. After everything he had done to get back home, a cab ride was going to screw him. "That your girl?" The driver asked.

"Uh, no," Ben said, thinking he caught the man's meaning. "Just a friend."

"Tell you what," said the driver. "I agree to wait on the money if your 'friend' rides up front, and stays while you go get it."

Ben immediately saw where things were going, and he didn't like it. He looked again at Lornamair, who met his eyes and subtly shook her head. This guy was the first person she had willfully laid eyes on, maybe ever, and it was possible that she was feeling shy. The idea amused Ben more than a bit. "She's actually pretty shy," Ben told the driver apologetically, hoping that it would be enough.

"Yeah, I bet she is," he said. They could both hear the grin form as he spoke.

"Listen, isn't there some way you could call your boss and verify that the ride is paid for? I'm sure that—"

"Nope, sorry," the driver said, not offering any further explanation. "I can drive back to the city and tell them to send another cab, if you want. It'll be awhile, though." Of course it would be awhile. The city was at least ninety minutes away, it was after midnight, Ben had no money on him, and the driver knew it. Which meant that the driver's offer wasn't an offer at all; it was an ultimatum. He wanted the pretty girl he saw in the back seat to ride in the front seat, and Ben doubted it was because he just wanted the company. And if he was the kind of guy who would take advantage of people so blatantly, then he was also the kind of guy who would do whatever he could to make sure they didn't get home at all that night if they didn't cooperate.

Screw this, Ben thought. He was anxious to get home, but not so anxious that he was about to let some punk hold the trip hostage in exchange for… whatever it was the kid thought he was going to get. He had no problem staying another night, and he was about to tell the driver so when Lornamair surprisingly spoke.

"I'll do it," she said. Ben whipped his head around in shock, only to find Lornamair staring at the driver calmly.

"Forget it," he told her. "We've been waiting already, another day isn't going to—"

"I *said* I'll do it," she shot back, her eyes carving paths through the unwitting driver's skull. It was then that Ben realized what was going down. Lornamair wasn't accustomed to how things were in the outside world, and she had probably never come across anyone who was as bold as the driver was being. That was why Ben had been pretty sure that his business-like advances had gone unnoticed by her. For some reason, though, he forgot that his emotionally telepathic friend would most likely feel something familiar when the driver's attention was on her— something that would, in all probability, sour the only good mood Ben had ever seen her in.

Ben didn't want to alarm the driver, so he tried to convey his message silently. He waved until she looked at him, and then distinctively mouthed the word "no," while his eyes told her that he meant it. Granted, the kid might have been a jerk, but he probably didn't deserve whatever it was that Lornamair was already cooking up. His message went unheeded as she mimicked his expression and just as distinctively mouthed the word "yes."

Then, aloud, she said, "Let's just get out of here. How do you work this?" Ben took a breath and reluctantly reached across her to get to the door handle. At least they wouldn't have to wait another day. Lornamair got out and studied the handle on the front door for a second before she figured out that lifting was the correct approach.

Ben watched with bated breath as his beautiful but deadly companion slid into the passenger's seat and pulled the door shut. The driver clearly liked what he saw before the interior light went out. "Damn," he remarked with a short laugh as Lornamair squirmed a bit to get comfortable. Ben rolled his eyes as she resituated the shirt on her shoulders and pulled her neckline up without actually moving it in a comically effective effort to get the driver to take note of her physique, as if he hadn't already. It was no longer a question of if, but how badly the kid was going to fall for Lornamair's bait—which, by extension, would determine just how badly the rest of his night was going to go.

Lornamair whipped her head just enough so that her hair fell and covered half of her face. She smiled sweetly to the driver and said, "May we go now?"

The driver, clearly comfortable around flirtatious women, nodded like there was a beat playing that only he could hear as he showed a wicked smile. "Let's do this," he said as he put the car in drive. A three point turn later, they were on their way home. *Well, maybe he* does *deserve it,* Ben thought to himself.

Five minutes down the road, Ben watched in silence as Lornamair seemed to be making idle conversation with their driver. He couldn't hear anything because the driver had closed the window that separated the front of the car from the back as soon as they had left, and the two were keeping their voices to a minimum. Lornamair was flirting shamelessly with him, and it would have bothered Ben if he hadn't known where it was headed. The poor kid was too brainwashed by his hormones to realize that her smiles were fake, and it was going to cost him, though Ben wasn't sure yet how much. She might let him off with a slap on the wrist; she was, after all, trying to turn over a new leaf. But what was the word that best described her? Deadly. Not beautiful and stern. Not beautiful and cranky. Beautiful and *deadly*. It was always very easy to see the beautiful, but no one ever saw the deadly until it was far too late. Maybe he should do the kid a favor and get him to stop the car and drop them off. Just tell him to send another cab out; they could wait right there for it on the side of a deserted highway. He knew that it would never happen, though. At that point, Ben knew that he was little more than an afterthought in the minds of both his new friend and the driver. They were busy talking, each with a very different idea of where that talking would lead to. Lornamair would want to finish the drive because she had something violent she wanted to do, and the driver would want to finish because he thought that he was going to get something that he was definitely not going to get. Whatever happened, Ben decided that he might as well get a ride home out of it.

People were incredible. This was the first member of Ben's "civilized" world that Lornamair had encountered up close (with the exception of his wife, who didn't do much to give her a great first impression, either), and she already had all the reasons she needed to hate him. As always, it really just boiled down to one. This man—this young, arrogant, presumptuous, chauvinistic, self-serving weasel—had the audacity to use their needs as leverage for the opportunity to have sex. That was always what it came back to, and this one had it emanating from him like smoke from a fire. It traveled across the front seat and hit her in pulsating waves of saturated lust, choking her insides with a panicky kind of heat that inexplicably registered as calm and confident at the same time. She realized that he thought he knew where things were headed, and the shock that she would put on his face when they got to where they were going was the only thing making his presence even tolerable. None of the women she had taken had felt this way. They had all made her sick, one way or another, but that was a direct result of her own feelings clashing with theirs. This man was truly disgusting, and she wondered if all men in the "civilized" world felt the same way. No, there was one in the back seat who hadn't bothered her at all. It briefly occurred to her that Ben wouldn't approve of what she intended, but he would have to forgive her this one infraction. External changes were much easier to make than internal ones, and so far, Lornamair had gone through the motions without actually being totally convinced of their merit. He would understand. Ben's emotions were subtler than those of most other people, but she knew that he didn't like the driver much either. She wondered if he knew what she knew. Maybe there was something in the driver's mannerisms that Ben recognized. She would have to remember to ask him later.

Lornamair smiled through the driver's emotional sewage and arched her back, feigning a tired stretch. She felt a single pulse of excitement as she did so, and thought about how easy it all was. Finding out what got pigs like this going was like playing a game of hot and cold. She would act, and then feel the reaction. If she gave it her undivided attention, she could determine everything through the unspoken messages that were carried on every human emotion. Lornamair wasn't a mind reader, but under circumstances like these, she was close enough. She could tell what he wanted to see, how he wanted to see it, and exactly when it would have the greatest effect. She could taunt him with it, torture him with it, and eventually drive him insane with it. It was no less than he deserved. And what would be the point? Ben would surely ask, if he could know what she was thinking. That part was simple. The more excited he got, the more sticky, revolting impulses she was forced to feel during the ride, then the more satisfying it was going to be to make him suffer when the time came to part ways.

"So what's with the clothes?" The driver asked.

Lornamair looked down at her roughly woven skirt and her primitive top and looked back up at him, playfully arching an eyebrow. "What's with them?" She asked.

"You look like a… like a… a jungle princess, or something."

"Are you nervous," she asked playfully, "now that you know you're in the company of royalty?"

"I would have expected a princess to have more jewelry," he said.

"Well how many princesses have you known?"

"Just one, now," the driver said, grinning. "You live around here?"

"I've lived in the village my entire life," she answered, rolling her eyes in false boredom.

"And now you wanna be a city girl, huh?"

"My friend back there thinks it'll be good for me," she said. "I'm not sure yet, but there's nothing wrong with trying new things, right?"

"I heard *that,"* he said with an easy smile, keeping his eyes on the road. "It's funny, though. You don't have an accent or anything like that. You don't even really dress like they do. It's like you were born to get outta there, right?"

"Yeah, maybe," she said, considering.

"So how long you known your friend?"

"Only about a week. He's giving me a place to stay, though."

"Oh yeah? You know what you wanna do for work?"

"I guess I haven't thought that far ahead," she told him, secretly beginning to regret her attire. Her clothes didn't interest him, for some reason. Her thighs were, for all intents and purposes, bare, and she knew for a fact her top flattered her profile. Granted, it had been a long time since she had thought about impressing anyone, but honestly, men never changed. Was it the burlap? No, wait, there it was... she had mistaken frustration for disinterest. That was much better. He was dying to know what she looked like without all that pesky clothing. This child was hers, with or without jewelry.

"Girl as good looking as you, you should be flaunting what you got, you know?" He asked rhetorically. "I know a guy on eighth who could hook you up with a nice gig if that's your thing."

Lornamair wasn't quite sure what he meant, but she knew a compliment when she heard one. "That's really sweet," she said, as though the driver had simply commented on her hairdo, and filing away the baffling use of the word "hook." Did he, or the "guy on eighth," have a hook they intended to use? She would like to see them try.

"Carlos," the driver said. "My name is Carlos."

"Carlos," Lornamair repeated. "What's a 'gig?'"

"Like a job, you know?"

Lornamair didn't know. "A job doing what?"

Carlos shrugged nonchalantly. "You know, do a little dance, make a little money…"

"A dance," she said. "Like for entertainment? Dance in front of people for entertainment?"

"Yeah, entertainment," Carlos said, still smiling like a shark who was confidently convincing his prey to follow him home. "We'd have to do something about those clothes, though."

Lornamair brought herself up to speed in a hurry, but continued to play dumb. "What's wrong with the ones I have now?" She asked innocently.

"They're not very entertaining," Carlos said. "I'm telling you, we trade that whatever-it-is you're wearing now for some leather knee-highs and a corset, you got more cash than you know what to do with." Not knowing what "nee-hyes" or "core-sets" were, or why she would want whatever "cash" was, Lornamair involuntarily envisioned herself in the most revealing thing she could think of and fought an impulse to crack Carlos's skull earlier than planned.

"You think I'm pretty enough?" She asked, doing everything but actually blushing.

"Oh, yeah," said Carlos, now looking away from the empty road and shamelessly sweeping his eyes from her head to her feet and back up again.

"And all I have to do is dance?" She pressed, asking with false interest.

"Well, maybe not *all* you do," said Carlos, again with that sly grin that ignorantly suggested that his quarry was oblivious to his intentions. "It depends on the money, right?" Money… *there* was a word she knew. God, what *wouldn't* people do for it?

"Yeah, I guess it does," Lornamair answered. She pretended to think for a moment, and then pretended to sound hopeful. "You could really get me that job? It sounds so easy and…fun."

"Yeah, sure, I can probably make that happen," Carlos said. "I tell you what—maybe you put in a little audition for me, I guarantee I can make it happen."

It was a monumental effort for Lornamair to prevent her face from mirroring her disgust. "Sounds fair," she said smoothly. "So when we get to where we're going, you just tell me what you want me to do, and I guarantee I can make *that* happen."

"Right on," Carlos said with a grin, sadly unaware that it might be his last.

When they reached the airport, Ben wasn't surprised to see that the driver had parked them almost as far from it as possible. He didn't know exactly what had gone on up front during the ride, but he did know what the driver had had in mind from the beginning, and he also knew that Lornamair would have done nothing to make him think otherwise— *if* she hadn't actually encouraged him. All it meant was that the driver was in danger, and he was definitely not aware of it.

Ben didn't really think that he was okay with leaving the kid to Lornamair's fancy, but what could he expect himself to do? There was no way to get him away from her without causing a scene, or at the very least upsetting the most dangerous girl he had ever met, and creating a scene at an airport was not something that he wanted to do. Besides, there was no reason to think that Lornamair was going to do anything worse than give him the beating of his life, and didn't he kind of deserve that? Who knew what the kid would have done if he had picked up two normal people and the girl wasn't as cooperative as Lornamair surely had been? Her actions had gotten them one step closer to home, and Ben thought that maybe he would be better off if he were to simply trust her instincts. His own, nevertheless, told him that he should find the driver's money and get back to them as quickly as possible.

He got out of the car and the barrenness of the parking lot confirmed the need for urgency. This was where they both wanted to be—away from witnesses. He looked down the lot at the airport and grimly noted that it seemed to be about a quarter of a mile away. At two in the morning, there weren't going to be enough people coming in to fill the lot and make them uncomfortable while he was gone, either. Lornamair would have more than enough time to wreak whatever havoc on the kid she pleased. Chilly air, an empty parking lot, and only the stoic overhead lamps as witnesses—an all-too-perfect murder scene.

Carlos rolled down his window and noted that Ben seemed noncommittal. "Go ahead, man, we'll be right here." Ben briefly thought about telling the kid that he was making a big mistake when Lornamair leaned over the console from the passenger's side and rested her head in her open palm. Her eyes told him everything. *We both know that this idiot deserves this,* they were saying. *Just go do what you have to do, and it'll be over before you know it. I might even let him live, if you really care that much.* "Hey man," Carlos interjected, "you owe me for the ride. She'll be fine right here." Lornamair raised her eyebrows and her smile was oh-so-slight. *If that isn't asking for it, I don't know what is.* She reached forward with her other arm and made a slow, shooing motion with the back of her hand. Ben turned quickly and walked with large strides toward the airport. "Take your time, huh?" Carlos called after him. "There's no fire." *You'd better hope it stays that way,* Ben thought to him.

A quarter-mile might have been a long estimate, but the walk was still long enough to make him cramp up a bit after keeping such a quick pace. Automatic doors, something Ben had all but forgotten about during his time off the coast of Luna, slid aside to let him through. The inside of the airport was grand and sprawling, a polar opposite of everything he had spent the last week of his life around. It actually felt good to see real civilization again, but Ben didn't have time to admire it. An ATM wasn't hard to find; the airport was sparsely populated with people reading to stay awake or not bothering to stay awake at all. He made a b-line for it and took out enough money to pay for the ride (which was, as Roger had warned, incredibly expensive), as well as a little extra for the trip. He started back toward the entrance before he had even stuffed it into his pocket, feeling good about the time was making. Even so, he was only half surprised to find Lornamair waiting for him when he exited the building. She worked awfully quickly when she wanted to.

There was an awkward pause. Her expression revealed nothing, and Ben felt obligated to ask. "Is he all right?"

"Of course not," she said.

Ben looked pointlessly out at the taxi, which was much too far away to tell him anything. At least it wasn't on fire. "What did you—"

"Do you really want to know?" Lornamair asked, taking a casual step toward him and placing her hands on his shoulders. Her eyes were sincere when she spoke. "You've had a rough enough week as it is."

Ben closed his eyes and found some resignation. "At least tell me he deserved it."

"He spoke to me as though I was an object," she said. "He wanted me to act like a whore, and he expected me to be grateful to him when he told me that he could get me a job actually *being* a whore. He even thought he could tell me how to express that gratitude. If I had been anyone else, I might have lived the rest of my life as a—what did he call it—a stripper. And he tried to convince me that it was all for *my* benefit. He deserved it."

"Is he alive?" Ben asked apprehensively.

The regret in Lornamair's voice was obvious. "Yes, he's alive. You're welcome."

"What if he alerts someone?"

"He won't." Ben knew Lornamair well enough to know that she didn't make claims she wasn't absolutely sure of.

"Well, I still owe him for the ride."

"No, you don't. My husband was good on his word. The ride was taken care of before he came to get us. He was only saying that to put us in a difficult situation. He probably would have let you pay him again, too."

Ben could only muster one response. "Wow," he said. "I guess you—"

"I beat it out of him, yes," she confirmed. "I *told* you, he deserved it." She looked back out toward the taxi and shook her head. "Generations later, they're all still so much the same."

Ben nodded and turned his head back toward the airport. He couldn't say for sure, but he doubted that any of Lornamair's myriad of books covered law. Really, there was no use in dwelling on it, or in arguing the technicalities of premeditated assault and battery with her. He briefly imagined how that conversation would go. *I don't know about you,* she would say, *but where I come from, we call that* justice.

"What's so funny?" Lornamair asked flatly, still gazing out at the car.

"Nothing," Ben said, although knowing that she felt the humor only made it funnier. "Are you ready to go?"

Lornamair stared at him a moment, unsure of whether or not the joke might be important, then let it go. She looked inside, crossed her arms like a child and set her jaw. Something was making her uneasy. "I don't know," she said. "It's so much in there. I can feel it all from out here. I don't think it feels good. It's all scrambled."

Ben didn't know why he hadn't thought of that already. She had never been around so many people before, and her emotions were probably going crazy. She was feeling distant hints of an entire airport's worth of happiness, jealousy, greed, anger, sadness, relief, and everything else that fell in the spectrum, and it would certainly get worse when she went inside. No wonder she was having second thoughts. "You can't turn it off, can you?" He asked her, knowing perfectly well what the answer would be.

"I never had to," she said, her voice beginning to tremble. "Is it like this all the time? With everyone?"

"I honestly don't know," Ben said. "But it looks like you're going to have to learn how to separate your own emotions from theirs."

"My own?" She said shakily. "What are my own?"

Ben smiled. "It'll be a whole new world for you when you find out."

Lornamair frowned and shook her head. "I don't know. Compared to this, Luna was paradise."

Ben considered a moment, then laughed out loud, prompting an uneasy look from his friend. "You know," he told her, "that's the same thing I thought."

"Maybe it'll change," she said, her eyes searching his and discovering something that seemed to set her mind at ease.

"Yeah, maybe." He took her hand and escorted her through the door and into a completely new life.